To Jessica,

Thanks for your help promoting my Doole. I see drinks in our future.

Alan McQueen
x

THE SUMMERVALE VOLUNTEERS

A NOVEL BY

ALAN McQUEEN

authorHOUSE®

AuthorHouse™ UK Ltd.
500 Avebury Boulevard
Central Milton Keynes, MK9 2BE
www.authorhouse.co.uk
Phone: 08001974150

First published by AuthorHouse 10/13/2008

ISBN: 978-1-4389-2441-0 (sc)
ISBN: 978-1-4389-2440-3 (hc)

Printed in the United States of America
Bloomington, Indiana

This book is printed on acid-free paper.

For Marie, Olivia and Elliott.

Thanks to Bob, Jan, Harold and Eileen. Thanks to
Vicky for the pictures and you for buying this.

CHAPTER ONE - COURT

The distinctive smell of the courtroom, the leather chairs, the sweat of a thousand backsides trembling at the thought of a guilty verdict and the long lonely walk down to the cells assails Alan Hitchcock's nostrils. But for Hitchcock (known to everyone as H) this time, the last time, the smell is rank, unpleasant, uninviting. Once the scent of a battlefield without bloodshed now more of a ruined castle with ghosts in every corner. Years of the smell meaning challenge; pitting his wits against an opponent, the smell of justice and integrity has now become a combination of body odour, bad breath and failure.

Lost in the reverie of times past Alan Hitchcock, smart but frayed, grey and drawn, older and wiser than he looks, but at 64, at the end of a career he has loved for more than forty years; a barrister, defender of rights and occasional drum beater for the oppressed, is startled to hear his name called.

"Mr Hitchcock. Are you joining us?" A call from the judge above wakes H from his daydream.

"Sorry your Honour."

"Your closing statement if you wouldn't mind."

Taking a deep breath, the smell filling him with one last surge of good intent, he takes a long hard look at the jury. His black robes flowing behind him, he strides toward the twelve jurors, his white court wig perched neatly atop his grey, distinguished head. Looking them directly in the eye he begins his summation of proceedings.

"I know you have heard the defendant to be a habitual criminal, and he was, make no mistake, but, please take note ladies and gentlemen, my use of 'was', rather than is. Yes, Maurice Claridge was, a thief, yes, Maurice Claridge did indeed break into the jewellers in Finchley, and yes, he was subsequently arrested trying to sell his ill-gotten gains at a car boot sale on Sunday morning in Romford, but, he has seen the error of his ways. The birth of his first grandson has changed his world view. He now has full time employment and a whole new perspective on life. He, at last, has a reason ***NOT*** to fight the system but to embrace it, to enter fully into the community and give his, now extended family, the full benefit of his time and energy. Incarceration will not benefit anyone in this case, he has admitted his guilt and is throwing himself on your mercy, this is a true case of redemption in times of callous, careless murder this man, once thief, has seen a route to a proper life and we should all help him take a step on that path and help him flourish into a decent citizen. Let's all do the right thing today and walk away from here with our heads held high having done the right thing. Ladies and gentlemen. Thank you."

H takes his seat next to his assistant, Elliott Longbottom; he looks 12 years old, barely shaving, barely out of law school but soon to oust H from the spot at the head of a trial. He looks at H with reverential wonder; he has seen a true artist at work. "Great speech, even the prosecution want to let him off."

"What a load of bullshit." H's smile only just concealing his true feelings. The young assistant unsure how, or indeed, if, to respond just stares at his older colleague.

Judge Romulus Armstrong (known among the law fraternity as "Rom Gone", as criminals being sentenced could expect a custodial sentence), presiding over events in Court Number 1 looks quietly around his court. A faux Scotsman with a beard like a small privet hedge, proud of the fact that in his judicial district he had put more people behind bars than any other judge. He smiles down on proceedings, his fingers steepled under his large grey beard. H thought it was like looking into your neighbours' hedge in the middle of a domestic row.

"Thank you Mr Hitchcock. An admirable summary of events as always. We shall miss your eloquent and impassioned pleas on behalf of your …er…clients."

Turning his full gaze on the gathered journalists and assorted family members of future cases, court junkies and wide-eyed law students Judge Armstrong addresses the court in full basso profundo voice.

"Ladies and gentlemen, sadly this is my learned friend's last case and I for one will miss the lyrical, heartfelt yet reasoned arguments he has delivered over many years."

Turning to the jury, he looks directly at the foreman, a balding bank teller from Stevenage wearing a v-necked sweater and a very bad bow tie.

"Have you the jury reached a verdict? "

Standing, the monk-like foreman replies. "We have your honour."

"What is it?"

"Guilty."

"Is this a unanimous decision?"

"It is."

"So be it, you may sit."

Turning to the dapper little man in the dock he continues

" Mr Claridge, your counsel has once again demonstrated his skill in a courtroom, you should be very grateful for his vibrant defence of your character. In as much as you have been found guilty, your record is appalling. A man of your age should not be climbing over fences and scaling walls to rob jewellers."

Maurice lifts his head and sounding not unlike Parker from Thunderbirds responds.

"No m'lud."

"By rights I should be sentencing you to a lengthy jail term. Your conviction sheet has done nothing to help save the rainforest with the amount of paperwork I have seen. I do, however, believe the statement made by Mr Hitchcock that you have seen the error of your ways and therefore I am prepared to take a chance on you. For once I am going to be lenient. I sentence you to five years." Maurice Claridge almost passes out and there is an audible gasp from some onlookers.

The Judge continues "… suspended, if you appear before this court on any charge you will disappear from view for a very long time. Do I make myself clear?"

"Yes your honour."

"Case dismissed. But before we leave I want to take this opportunity to bid a fond farewell to Mr Hitchcock, a much admired colleague and stout defender of lost causes for many, many years. I will miss the eloquent defence mustered for many unworthy of his talent; I feel a part of this courtroom will be leaving when he goes. Au revoir Mr H. We'll take lunch now. Court will reconvene in one hour."

With a bang of his gavel, Judge Armstrong draws proceedings to a close and the court quickly starts to empty. Young lawyers, court officials, press personnel and family and friends of the defendants and witnesses all file out. A swift exit and soon H is left with just a briefcase and a hungry looking young lawyer.

"What next then?" Elliott enquires as he puts a sheaf of papers in his sleek, shiny black briefcase.

H puts his papers in a battered brown leather briefcase that could have been used 100 years earlier and not been out of place. Then he stops, removes the file and hands it to Elliott. "Here. You take them back; I'll give you the final papers when I'm done with Maurice, that way I don't need to go back to the office."

"Not even to say goodbye."

"Elliott, you have so much to learn. They have kicked me out. I am not waving a fond farewell and trotting off to a new life in Provence to paint and make my own wine. I have been shafted, knifed in the back, and the front and sides for that matter; they don't want an old fart like me cluttering up their shiny offices. Since that knobhead Fitzsimons took over it's a factory. How many hours can you book, what more can you screw out of your clients? It's a bit like being a battery hen. You're kept in the dark, fed and watered enough to stay alive but you're up to your knees in your own piss and shit. Eventually the smell is unbearable even for you but you've no way to escape. You just wait for the relief of death. I joined this firm, or what it once was, in 1966 straight from law school. I wanted to be a free range hen, to run through the trees looking for my own adventures. I loved my work and the way we conducted it. We made a difference; I wanted to make a difference. They don't have time to listen to their clients; they don't want old roosters like me shitting in their yard. Do you understand?"

Elliott looks really confused.

"You want to be a chicken farmer?"

Shaking his head H smiles "Fucking Jamie Oliver has a lot to answer for."

H picks up his battered old briefcase and takes one last long look around. Turning a full 180 degrees, the memories flooding back once again.

With a sigh he walks towards the large double doors knowing he will never set foot in the courtroom again.

CHAPTER TWO - CELLS

The cement steps leading down to the basement of the court building are cold and noisy as H's footsteps echo loudly. He turns a corner and the police officer guarding the door nods in his direction. There is not much love lost between defence barristers and the police, if the police mess up an investigation the defender will jump all over the mistake and then it's seen as though the defender is on the side of the criminal. The more experienced officers all know Alan Hitchcock to be on the side of justice. He always played by the book, never belittled a rookie officer and tried to work with the police. The nod was recognition of many years of verbal jousting and a grudging respect. H thought " what would it be like if they hated me?"

The interior of the holding cell is exactly as depicted in The Sweeney circa 1979; grey walls, a single table, Formica topped, two battered old wooden chairs and little else. H, or Mr H to many of his clients, sat opposite Maurice filling in the relevant release forms. Maurice takes out an old rusting tin, flips the lid and removes a skinny roll-up cigarette.

"OK if I smoke Mr H?"

"Crack on Maurice, not much point in me living the healthy life now, and even if it's against the rules now it means we're in the right place to break them!"

An equally ancient lighter fires the small cancer stick into life, and Maurice shifts to the side and crosses his legs, his finger removing a small crumb of tobacco from his tongue.

"Is this really your last day Mr H?"

Hitchcock looks up with a resigned expression.

"Yes Maurice, they want young blood in Armani suits, sharp haircuts and blunt brains. Processors and deal brokers, the law is of secondary consideration. I am too old to change my ways and since the witch took the house, the car, my money and my suits I, the defender of the innocent, and not so innocent……."

Smiling at Maurice.

"…..the arbiter of justice and legal precedent has been cast aside like a worn out shoe with only dog shit for company. The razor sharp adolescent geniuses will plea bargain; deal and expense account every case and sod the consequences. Maurice, they would have done a deal to get you three years if they didn't need to go to court and state your case!"

Maurice blows a tatty smoke ring. "Bugger."

"Bugger off more like. They don't give a shit about anyone my age. No pension, she had that, no job, no prospects, no house, she had that too. Bugger doesn't really cover it."

"So where are you going to go next Mr H?"

"Oh life is good, I will be an inmate at the excitingly named SummerVale, a retirement home for……the nearly deceased, dry and dusty decrepit sad and crusty old farts that no-one wants or can be bothered with."

H looks at the face of the old lag in front of him, a career criminal who is about to go home to a loving family, new Grandson and be welcomed with open arms, yet he, who has never done a dishonest turn in his life is about to be cast into the pit of despair that is an old people's home.

He smiles.

"Sorry to be so sour Maurice, I'm not really that bitter and twisted………..well, not quite twisted."

Maurice leans forward, cupping his roll-up inside his hand and looks from side to side almost furtively.

H looks around.

"What?"

"Mr H, you've always done right by me, kept me out of stir a few times and especially this last time. It is the last time you know, I'm off the books, through the long grass. I swear down, and now my little 'un has popped her first sprog out I want to be there for him, the little ankle biter, I want to watch what I can of him growing up, I wasn't there much for my three, but I aim to be a decent Grandad. As I live and breathe Mr H, I'm done with it. Finito. From now on I'm as straight as a very straight thing that's got no twists in it. And just to prove it, you know I spoke to you about the golden touch I'd one day pull, well it ain't never gonna happen. I'm gonna tell you a story, as old Maxey Bygraves used to say, and when I'm done you'll believe I'm never playing again. "

"I believe you now Maurice."

"Nah, you wanna believe, but this will convince. Remember, wealth is freedom Mr H, wealth is freedom. So, I found out a secret, a secret rich people keep from scallywags like me. They hate paying tax.!

"No shit Sherlock."

"Mr H, I mean they **really** hate paying tax and will do almost anything to avoid it. But I discovered just one of their scams."

Maurice inches forward in his seat, now just inches from H's nose.

"Back in the 60's I started off doing jewellers, easy to fence and the toffs couldn't resist buying another bracelet or necklace. I got good at it, got myself a reputation. They used to call me Sparkles. I really had the diamond touch. Well, over the years I worked a few of the better areas in London, in the nineties I moved upmarket and one night I did a place in Chelsea, nice little gaff down a quiet side street, the result wasn't great but I found a lovely leather folder which I swiped. When I got it home and had a butchers it contained details of a delivery to be made the following week. A crate of stuff, not only diamonds but gold, cash, documents all sort of gear".

H frowns, wondering where this is going, but intrigued enough to keep listening.

Maurice continues "Every month, the last Thursday of every month to be precise, a small plane, a 12 seater, with extra baggage capacity lands at Shoreham airport, that's near Lancing."

"I know where Shoreham is."

"Good. It's a small airport with very little activity. But at 10.45 that morning this small plane lands, it taxis to the hangar and takes on board a large wooden crate, sometimes two, but never more than three. Occasionally a couple of passengers, but rarely."

"What's the point of this Maurice?"

"Bear with me Mr H, it's a good story and one I've never been able to tell anyone. So, the plane lands, a little Pilatus PC-12, it loads, re-fuels and takes off again all within 45 minutes tops. This plane then flies directly to Switzerland where the contents of the crate, or crates, are deposited in numbered Swiss Banks in Zurich, out of the clutches of our Chancellor of the Exchequer. My plan was to acquire a plane I could disguise as the one they expect, land early, load the goodies and fly off to a small abandoned airfield and Bob's your Uncle, Fanny's your Aunt the loot is lifted and I was off to warmer climes. Greatest part was, they can't call the cops 'cos they are at it themselves. It's a good plan, just rich people hiding their wealth, they won't even miss it."

Silence in the small room. H's hand is motionless in mid-air as though he was about to say something.

"Well?"

"Great plan Maurice, no wonder you spent so much time in the nick."

Maurice sighs.

"It is a good plan Mr H, just never had the readies to buy a second-hand plane, and find someone to fly it, but there you go. The take would have been over half a mil plus gold, jewellery all sorts of dodgy gear. All my books and plans, details and tape recordings are in a lock box at the back of Willy's Washeteria, a launderette on the corner of Cordelia Street and Augusta Street in E14."

Maurice reaches into his pocket and removes a key on a chain and an envelope; he places both on the table.

"That's the key, Box 319 and all the basic details. Inside the box are detailed maps and a lot more info, the best blag ever organised. Now I can't ever do the job and you will be my guardian angel."

H looks at the key, the envelope and back at Maurice and smiles.

"That's good news Maurice; prison is no place for a Grandad. How did you know you were going to get off? You must have had this all planned – including your speech – so that's interesting. But most important why keep it in a washeteria?"

"I knew you'd do the business Mr H, 'cos you're the best. Yes, I'd decided to jack it in even if I went down so thought I'd tidy up a few loose ends and well, the washeteria is the only place to launder money Mr H."

H laughs in spite of himself.

He takes the key chain and puts it around his neck, drops the key inside his shirt, places the bulky envelope in his jacket pocket and stands.

"I'll hang on to these, keep you out of trouble and ensure the law of the land is upheld."

"Thanks Mr H. If you happen to go to Willy's ask for Costas, he looks after the lock-box office. You can't miss him, he's a six foot seven, twenty six stone monster bubble that keeps the peace and makes sure everyone's gear is safe."

"Maurice, I'll never need to go there, I have no idea what a six foot seven bubble is but I'll keep these safe as a reminder of a life redeemed."

A key rattles in the door and a guard opens it and sticks his head in. "Ready?" He enquires.

"Oh yes." H and Maurice answer together.

CHAPTER THREE - DEPARTURE

Alone in his rented flat, H looks round the room. Chipboard wallpaper, MFI furniture, an easy chair with a striped green cover and a crocheted head rest. He looks at the picture of a small boy with a tear running down his face and shakes his head a little. This morbid little room has been home (if you could call it that) for two and a half years, well two years and seven months actually, well thirty one months, well actually, one hundred and twenty seven weeks to be precise. Not that it had played on his mind of course. The six bedroom detached house in Weybridge with the beautiful lawn nurtured over twelve years with the fruit trees and quiet reading area he had built in the corner of the herb garden seemed a lifetime away. The fact that he had been forced to live in this pit of mind numbing boringness for the last years of his working life really, really got to him.

"Wealth is freedom." He says aloud. Then caught himself looking in the mirror. Where did that come from?

"Bloody hell H, you are losing it."

He picks up his battered suitcase, the wheelie case with his few possessions and his old brown briefcase takes a final look around and walks out into the hallway. Shutting the door behind him he descends the stairs with difficulty, the bags banging against the flowery wallpaper. At the front door he hands his key to the agent waiting and without a word, departs.

A short walk to his car, a beautiful 1990 racing green Jaguar XJS convertible. The only possession he managed to hang on to in his divorce settlement, and that's only because 'The Witch' found it difficult to get in and out of – due to the fact that her arse is wider than the seat – according to H lately anyway.

The car was immaculate. Cream leather interior, walnut dashboard. H loves his car.

Depositing the bags in the boot, H climbs inside and starts the engine. A deep rumble and a throaty roar makes him feel at last he is somewhere familiar and friendly. He looks up at the dingy flat, first window, first floor, in a grey undistinguished building. He presses the cd button and smiles as Bachman, Turner, Overdrive flood the car with "You Ain't Seen Nothing Yet", a rueful smile "Let's hope not." And he pulls away from the kerb and heads toward his new life.

The sun is shining but it is not hot, early March sunshine, no winter so far and an unusually warm start to spring. H decides to put the top down and feel the breeze blowing away the cobwebs from his mind. Merging onto the M3 he hears a plane and looks up as a small twin engine plane drones overhead, he looks at it carefully, the wingspan almost directly overhead, the number on its side clearly visible and the pilot quite clear in the cockpit. "Wealth is freedom."

He looks back down as the traffic slows to a complete halt. Fumes surrounding him from the large trucks and 4x4's alongside.

"Piss off Maurice and leave me alone."

He flicks a switch and the roof comes up, once again he is in his own little world.

The M3 snakes forward, at best H manages 40mph, the traffic ahead seemingly endless.

The driving rock anthems blasting out of the music system keeping him drumming his fingers on the walnut steering wheel. His mind is somewhere closer to the sea though.

Suddenly the cars in front begin to move quicker, the vans and lorries revving hard as a slight incline keeps their speed down, H sees a sign for Junction 6 so he indicates and glides onto the slip road. A smooth transition onto anther A road and he's heading for the A31. H pulls into a lay-by to look at his map. Although he had done the journey once before he is unsure of any landmarks. Picking up signs for Worldham Park he heads for Wyck, a small hamlet that he knows will guide him to SummerVale. He had glumly surmised that this place would indeed get on his Wyck and decided very quickly never to crack that joke as it was not very funny and almost everyone would have used it before.

Driving through Wyck is a speedy exercise, only a few houses to see in a very brief flash through the hamlet and he was through the other side. As he turns a gentle curve a large wall running alongside the grass verge hints at an estate beyond. H slows to 30mph and sees a sign ahead, a white triangle with a red outline, two old people with sticks denoting 'old/disabled people crossing'. A very common sight near to an old people's home. What is unusual is the aged gentleman in a tatty black tracksuit holding the sign with one hand and spray painting a penis onto the old gent in the sign with the lady's hand extended from behind. H thought it was quite well done. He lowers his window as he pulls alongside.

"Oi Banksy. SummerVale?"

The spray-painter glowers at H.

"First turning, welcome to hell."

"You missed a bit. Be lucky."

The old gent calmly turns away, giving H the finger as he does so.

H drives another 100 yards and a large open gate appears in the high wall. He turns in and crunches across the gravel drive. He drives along a tree lined avenue, slowly. He glances from side to side seeing no-one, taking in the beautiful lawn and well kept flower beds. A large imposing manor house looms into view and H pulls up outside. He parks to one side of the turning circle and stares up at the ivy covered entrance and the sign above the grand oak door – **SUMMERVALE** - his shoulders slump as the realisation of his new circumstances are brought fully into focus. H opens his door as the entrance to SummerVale swings open and an attractive woman in her early 40's rushes out. She is wearing a white nurse's coat and sensible shoes.

"Move that bloody heap, can't you damn well read?"

H looks at the sign she is pointing to. H sums up the situation and turns into Alistair Sim in an instant, adopting the upper class accent and mannerisms portrayed in School For Scoundrels.

"Actually no, I'm illiterate, what does it say my dear?"

The nurse moves closer and glares at H.

"Are you serious? are you making fun of me?, do you know who I am?, are you supposed to be here?, where have you come from?"

"No, yes, no, yes, the dark side of the moon."

"What?"

"No, I'm not being serious, I can read. Yes, I was making fun of you, no, I have no idea who you are but looking at the coat either you are the painter, it is an equal opportunities world after all, or a nurse of some kind. Yes I unfortunately am supposed to be here, and I have travelled many miles from London town to be with you. I followed a bright star in the sky, I bring you not gold or incense but mirth."

"What on earth are you gabbling on about? Who are you? And please, just one answer will do."

"My name is Alan Hitchcock and I am to be a resident at this fine establishment. Where should I park my vehicle?"

"Oh, we were expecting you this morning. Did you get lost?"

"Held up by the great British traffic but I'm here now. Should I move or can I unload the car first?"

"Bring your things in then park it round the back, there are loads of spaces, very few have cars here."

"Thank you."

H looks at the back of the nurse who hasn't introduced herself or offered any help with his bags.

"Satan's little helper."

The nurse turns on her heel.

"Pardon me?"

H looks sheepishly at the floor.

"Oh.....nothing. I'll bring my bags."

H opens the boot of his Jaguar and takes out his cases and briefcase and follows the quickly disappearing rear of the SummerVale nurse.

CHAPTER FOUR - ARRIVAL

The entrance hall to SummerVale is a throwback to Victorian times. A vast open space with wood panelling everywhere. As H steps inside, the white–clad harpie eyes him suspiciously. She is holding a clip-board with a number of sheets of paper on top.

"Hitchcock."

"Mister Hitchcock, yes, that's me."

She glares at him for a beat.

"Hitchcock. Room 68."

H smiles like a naughty schoolboy.

"Shame, do I get sixty nine next year if I'm a good boy?"

"No, 68 is your room from now on until…"

"I snuff it?"

"Until further notice, sign here" She thrusts the clipboard under H's nose, he signs in the appropriate place and ceremoniously hands her pen back, she snatches it and turns on her sensible heel and sets off toward the stairs.

"Follow me."

H throws a Nazi salute at her back and she looks over her shoulder and he quickly turns it into a scratch of his armpit but they both know he's been seen.

He grabs his bags and lugs them after her. Up one broad flight of stairs and through a swing door until they reach the end of a carpeted hallway. She stops outside Room 68. She takes a key from the clipboard and inserts it. Pushing the door open she stands back and ushers H into the room. He walks in with a weak smile and looks at the single bed, single tatty chair and Ikea wardrobe. He drops his briefcase on the bed and stands the case up. He turns to look through the window, a nice view of the lawn and trees; away in the distance he can see some sheep and horses.

He turns around and the Nurse has stepped into the room.

"A few rules."

"JaVol."

"What?"

"Nothing."

"No smoking in the room. No cooking in the room. We encourage residents meet in the lounge, it helps integrate newcomers and stimulate conversation and activity. As you are state provided you get clean sheets once a week, your room will be cleaned on Mondays. No extra heating appliances."

She appears to be ticking off a mental sheet. H is non-plussed.

"Can I sleep in here?"

She glowers over her clipboard.

"Very funny."

"Look Miss…..?"

The Nurse looks daggers at him.

"Do you have a first name?"

"Nurse."

H turns on the full charm; he needs this woman on his side.

"Come on now, we've gotten off on the wrong foot. I'm a bit frazzled from the drive and change in lifestyle, you're obviously a bit stressed, I don't know the rules and I'm really going to rely on you for decent conversation, information and mental stimulation. It would appear that you are to be my saviour, so may I know your first name......please?"

Softening.

"Olivia, but everyone refers to me as Nurse Phipps. I'm the on-site Nurse, there is a full time Warden, Mrs. Hailsham but she is more involved in the administration than welfare of the residents. The handbook on the dresser..."

She points to a plastic file on the Formica top – "will explain everything."

She turns to leave.

"Breakfast is eight 'til ten. Lunch twelve thirty prompt and dinner at six thirty. The toilet is fitted with an alarm cord, just pull it and we'll be there very quickly. Unpack your stuff and meet me in the lounge, that's down the stairs and through the double doors to the right. I'll show you around and introduce you to the residents. Okay?"

Smiling. "Thanks Olivia."

She smiles back.

"See you downstairs."

Nurse Phipps leaves and pulls the door closed behind her leaving H alone in his new home.

He sits on the edge of the bed and surveys the room. He stands with a sigh and flips the catch on his briefcase, leaving it on the bed. He lifts the large case onto the side of the bed and starts to unpack his clothes.

Just ten minutes later and H has relocated his clothes to the wardrobe and chest of drawers.

"Well that didn't take long." He says as he puts the empty case on top of the wardrobe.

Opening the door H pokes his head gently round the corner. "Boo!"

H jumps back and almost soils his chinos. "What the fuck?"

H, breathing hard leans out into the corridor - he looks into the smiling face of a bushy haired, professorial face. Black rimmed glasses, fluffy Denis Healy eyebrows, rosy cheeks, deep blue smiling eyes. The face is grinning back at H.

"You ok? "

H steps out into the corridor and stands in front of the other resident.

"Didn't mean to make you jump."

"Jump? I almost shit myself. I would've been known as the incontinent inmate! Great start."

Bushy face laughs. "I like you already. I'm George."

He puts out a large gnarled hand and H shakes it. A firm manly handshake, telling a tale in its intensity. A proper handshake not some wet-dead-fish handshake like some of the lawyers H had met in his working life. He shook the hand back equally firmly and smiled back at the happy face in front of him.

"I'm Alan....Hitchcock......H to most...er...friends."

"Nice to meet you H."

The handshake ends and they are standing in the corridor. H in his chinos and v necked jumper, converse baseball boots and looking cool and quite trendy, George in loud checked trousers, a striped shirt and spotted cravat. He looks like an explosion in a paint factory.

H looks George up and down

"Well, we won't lose sight of you will we."

"Funneeeeeeee, I have no-one to impress with my sartorial elegance so I just grab the nearest item and if they clash.....who cares. Come on, I'll show you around."

George sets off toward the stairs with H in hot pursuit.

They walk down side by side and see Nurse Phipps waiting at the bottom.

"Oh God, Ratshit."

H looks around on the floor.

"Where. That's gross."

George nudges H and nods at the Nurse. He leans closer to H.

"Her. We call her Ratshit, you know, One Flew Over The Cuckoos Nest, Nurse Ratched, we call her Ratshit. But not in ear-shot."

H smiles at the reference.

"Is it me or is she wrapped a bit too tight?"

George leans ever closer.

"Tighter than a ducks bum. She's ok really but needs to lighten up."

The two men come to the bottom of the stairs still smiling. Nurse Phipps approaches them.

"You look like two naughty schoolboys, what are you up to?"

George replies for them both. "Just discussing films we love."

She looks very sceptical.

"Can you show Mister Hitchcock around please George; nearly everyone has gone into the village for the Twin Town celebrations so it will be a bit quiet."

George responds "It's always quiet."

H enquires "What Twin Town celebrations?"

George takes H by the arm and guides him in the direction of the lounge H had spotted earlier.

"Yeah, the local town is twinned with Amityville, except there's more fun in Amityville and they are having a fifty year parade, party and free drinks, hence the residents get ferried down there for a free sherry and a hotdog."

"Whoopee-doo."

George realises he has a new friend to help him through the days ahead and smiles.

"Come on, I'll show you round."

After a quick tour of the facility, an explanation of where he can and can't go H takes his leave of George and heads back to his room. As he gets to the stairs Nurse Phipps appears from nowhere.

"All ok?"

H spins round. Smiles.

"Yes thanks Olivia, it's fairly straightforward."

She smiles a little.

"Excellent. I am sure you will be very happy here."

H weighs up this assumption.

"Only time will tell." He pauses, and then continues "But I hope so."

H ascends the stairs and closes the door to number 68 and lies down on his bed and stares at the ceiling until sleep comes.

CHAPTER FIVE - GEORGE

H opens the door to his room, steps into the antiseptic smelling hallway, empty and quiet. Walking slowly on the rug covered floor, his leather soles clattering if he steps onto the wood beside the carpet each step taking him further into unknown territory, so much that he slows his walk and steps gingerly with each foot. An unsettled night has left H feeling more than a little weird, his dreams are still fresh and he is trying to adjust to his new surroundings. He descends the stairs slowly, taking in the pictures, the faded carpet and the polished banister as he runs his hand down it. He arrives at the common room, and peers through the glass partitioned door to a sight that turns his blood cold. A room covered in bad carpet, old chairs around the walls occupied by even older people, a scene that reminds H of a dance for ancient wallflowers, no-one willing to dance. People with no life, no spark. Grey people in various stages of decline, the living dead.

H reaches down toward the handle when a tap on his shoulder makes him jump out of his skin.

"Shit."

He looks round and George is standing there grinning, dressed in pyjamas, an old wool dressing gown and slippers.

"You creep up on people like Nosferatu. You nearly gave me a bloody heart attack….again. Make some noise when you're behind me."

H glances down at Georges slippers, checked and practical.

"Dancing shoes?"

"Brothel creepers they aren't." smiling, George opens the door.

"Let's go and see if any of them are still alive."

H follows George into the room; the faint drone of Distant Drums can be heard as they walk across the empty centre of the room.

"I feel like I've been put in a crypt before I'm dead. Have you got a mirror handy?"

George turns, smiling quizzically "You look fine, what do you need a mirror for?"

"To check if any of them are still breathing!"

"Come and have some breakfast and meet some people."

"Live ones?"

"You never know, most are just dormant, like volcanoes."

"Volcanoes throw up lava, not dribble their lunch down their fronts!"

"Let's go see the chess boys."

H puffs his cheeks out. "Oh great, the inertia Olympics."

"You'll be surprised; they even stand up once in a while."

"They should be fucking careful."

They walk to a table by the window. Two men are playing chess. A white haired black man of indeterminate age, stocky but still fit looking, is sitting opposite a pony-tailed white man with a wispy beard and bushy eyebrows; they are both staring at the board.

The quartet is frozen in time for a couple of minutes, no-one moving or saying anything. The pony tailed man reaches forward and moves his bishop two places forward diagonally. Still neither man looks up.

George puts his hands in his dressing gown pockets. "Gentlemen, this is H, a new inmate."

Pony Tail looks up and smiles hello and nods at the black man opposite.

"This is Gus, ex-flyer, defender of the realm, bad chess player, Yorkshireman to the core, a loser in love and lover of losing. I'm Gilbert."

Before H can respond, and without looking up Gus responds, sounding like a black Brian Glover. "Only part of that is true. I rarely lose to the happy hippy here."

H peers through the window at the lawn outside, wishing he was out there.

"Nice to meet you both. Do you guys play a lot?"

Gilbert looks at H as if he's just insulted his Mother.

"Every day. Gus here is always white, I am always black, and it helps redress the racial imbalance in the world. Do you play?"

H smiles uncomfortably. "Very badly…..nice values but what happens when you play Monopoly?"

"We remove Mayfair as no-one in here could afford it anyway, Whitechapel and Whitehall become beige and life is good unless we go to jail."

Gilbert reaches his hand out and Gus gives him a sideways swipe. An exchange between two old men acting like teenagers.

"'Tis true my man and tell it to the judge."

H and George head off to a free table without another word and sit. H is still shaking his head as he sits and looks out of another window.

"Wealth is freedom."

George furls his bushy eyebrows. "What?"

"Oh nothing, just a mantra from an old lag I once knew."

H and George sit in two old chairs away from the rest of the inmates.

H has a startled look on his face. He watches as two old men walk by in the direction of the windows. As they pass H hears them exchange just a few words:

"Turdbreath."

"Wankpot."

"Pussknob."

"Arsepart."

"Shagnasty."

They fade away as they near the window clearly still exchanging pleasantries.

H looks at George.

"What was all that about?"

"Oh, that's just Percy and Ken. They were best of mates in here for years then Ellen arrived, an elderly widow woman who played them both. Percy thought he had secured her heart then she moved on to Ken, they fell out over her. She moved on, actually she did more than that, she found a rich old boy and got married to him and left here in a Rolls Royce. So Percy and Ken started hurling insults at each other, and that's all they ever do now even though they play crib against each other every day."

"George old son, this place is double strange, with a side order of strange and an extra large strange for dessert. Herman Munster, Gomez Addams and the cast of Rocky Horror would all love it here."

H glances round the room. A collection of grey faces, dry, wrinkly, old faces. Sad faces. Few smiles and little conversation and not because of the early hour.

"Does it ever liven up here?"

George cocks his head to one side "Oh yeah, on Wednesday they play bingo and once a month Ronnie Gale and his Magic Organ entertain us to within a hairs breadth of our life. Songs from the Jim Reeves catalogue and an occasional tune once made popular by Richard Clayderman or Russ Conway, except he murders them! "

"Oh my God, I can't wait for that. And what did you do in the real world before the onset of the grey death?"

George puts his hands out in front of him and wiggles his fingers.

"A pianist, nice, where did you play?"

George smiles.

"No, I was a computer analyst, a specialist. Trained all these little wannabe geeks until they could do the work half well. I taught them a USB from an STD and they gave me a P45. Typical."

H furrows his brow.

"How good were you?"

"Not so much of the past tense pal. I'm still the business on a laptop. Keep my hand in by hacking into Ratshit's computer and changing her schedule and prescription orders. She has no idea who's doing it but has threatened to neuter the person responsible if she ever catches them."

"Can you order me some medicinal scotch?"

"I doubt it but I'll see what I can do."

H looks across at two ladies in the corner playing cards and nibbling toast. Neither seemed to have brushed their hair for a decade, both are reading magazines as well as munching on toast at the same time as they played cards.

H nods in their direction.

"What's with The Andrews Sisters?"

George grins at the war-time reference.

"More like the Witches of Eastwick, except they are only two. Trisha and Margaret, not Maggie, Mags or Marge, it has to be Margaret. They play cards every day, scrabble on Friday and Saturday and always sit in the same seats. They never get any visitors and have been here for years. I heard a story that Margaret, she's the one in the electric blue trouser suit, lost everything to a con-man. Her husband died and she was all alone, an insurance guy called and made friends, over the next six months he visited almost every day and convinced her to make a few investments.

The first couple worked and then he tapped her up for a big investment, enough to make retirement easy. She has two kids so with the extra money they could both have a house. She re-mortgaged, gave this shit-bag the money, he of course disappeared never to be seen again. She had to sell her house, the kids got nothing so in a fit of greedy outrage they abandoned her and she ended up here as part of a card-playing duo that never gets a visit, never smile and just about survive on tea and toast every day."

"Nice people in the world eh?"

"Yeah, the weak and vulnerable are always fair game for these toe-rags."

"What about Michelle Pfeiffer?"

"Ah, Trisha, an equally tragic story. She lost her husband to cancer and re-married a younger man who proceeded to dismantle her life, offload her assets and run up massive debts in her name. He stayed until the money ran out and shot off like a scalded cat when she couldn't pay for their lifestyle anymore. She hates men with a vengeance and will be prickly as a porcupine even if she knows nothing about you. Shame really, two old biddies that the world turned over then turned its back on them."

H sighs "We are the silent minority, an unwanted addition to the economy of the world. They make drugs to keep us alive, make us last longer then find more and more ways to make our existence unpleasant."

"What can we do? Unless you have wads of cash life is tough." George shrugs his shoulders and starts to roll a cigarette.

"Wealth is freedom."

George looks at H, furrows his eyebrows "That's the second time you've said that, what does it refer to?"

H smiles.

"I don't know yet, but I might need to find out. Fancy a cuppa? "

H stands to go and get the drinks. He looks down at George and smiles.

"You're a Londoner aren't you?"

"Born and bred, west, West Hampstead.....or Kilburn when I lived there."

"I need to ask you something. What's a six foot seven monster bubble?"

George laughs

"Not someone you'd want to meet in a dark alley."

None the wiser, H sets off for the tea urn as George laughs in the background.

CHAPTER SIX - THINKING

Back in the quiet of number sixty eight, H opens the envelope Maurice had given him in the cells under the court. The instructions are written in an uneven hand, not typed. A brief outline of the story Maurice had told H, a few extra details about the flight, destination, and possible content of the crates. On the reverse is a hand written map of the airport, a very detailed map with roads, building heights (H supposed Maurice was used to judging heights if he had to scale a wall) fences, security details, some phone numbers and a list of contacts.

On a second sheet is a map leading to Willy's Washeteria in East London. The name Costas, a phone number and a note written underneath in a red pen. It was a note for him:

If you're reading this Mr H then things have got pretty bad or pretty dull for you. I always thought you were a great bloke, and I hope you follow this plan through. Talk to Costas, you can't miss him; he'll steer you right and get all the stuff from my lock-box. It'll cost you £100 but it'll be worth it. Ask Costas if you need anything else. He owes me a favour or two.

Good luck Mr H.

Best

Maurice

H shakes his head as he reads the note.

"You crafty old bugger."

H removes a legal pad from his briefcase and flips it open. He stares at the blank page his pen poised above it. Ten minutes later he has made four flower like squiggles and drawn a cartoon cat.

H stands and walks around his small room. What does he know about doing a robbery? Nothing. What would happen if he got caught? Prison. Who would care? No-one. Who could help him? George? Maybe. Gus? Maybe. Gilbert? Maybe. The others are all comatose. Most can't tie their shoelaces let alone tie up a security guard if need be.

"What are you thinking about you twerp, who do you think you are Tony Soprano. Twat. And you're talking to yourself. Aarrgghh."

He puts all the papers together in a pile and tucks them into the legal pad and places them in his briefcase, closes it and puts it on the floor beside his chair.

He clicks the TV remote and a black and white shot of Sterling Hayden fills the screen, he is by a fence at the airport right at the end of The Killing, a small dog runs across the tarmac, the luggage cart swerves, a case tumbles off and thousands of dollars blow in the wind across the ground.

"Oh shit." H thinks it's a conspiracy.

He turns the TV off again and picks up the paper. Front page is a story about a diamond heist in Hatton Garden, thieves got away with 2 million pounds worth of jewels, and police think it was an inside job. He turns the page and there is a story about a knight of the realm exposed for fraudulently obtaining land that rightfully belonged to his employees. He faces a prison sentence and being stripped of his knighthood.

"Jesus, they're all at it."

His head spinning H lies on the bed and covers his face with the thin pillow. He lays quite still for over an hour then sits bolt upright.

"No harm in finding out."

He starts with his legal pad, he makes notes:

> SHOREHAM airport
> Cars
> George?
> Gilbert?
> Gus? (pilot)
> Percy x
> Ken x
> Trisha?
> Margaret?
> Nurse Phipps (how to avoid)
> Money
> Maps
> Plane?????
> Hideaway

His hand hovers over the page, he is calm, he is focussed, and he knows it'll never happen but he can have fun outlining the possibility. He decides to explore the dark side, see what could be achieved. Where to start?

Picking up the letter from Maurice he starts to make notes about location, the plane's potential content, timings, dates (looking in his diary) a list of roads and turnings. Warming to his task he starts to compile a 'to do' list and quickly realises he is short on information about many aspects of this job. He likes to think of it as a job, not a blag, not a robbery but a job.

He decides he needs to make a few purchases and grabs his wallet, slips on some shoes and heads for the door.

Walking into a large PC World usually fills him with dread, spotty geeks talking cyber talk with no explanation. This time he knows exactly what he wants. He picks out a very light Viao laptop, a compatible printer, a top end Sony video camera and a high spec Minolta camera with a zoom lens. He hands his credit card to Ravi the helpful assistant and departs with a free carry case and a laptop bag along with his purchases.

Back at number sixty eight he starts to open his parcels, discarding the wrapping and foam packaging on the floor as he sets up his new equipment. He plugs the laptop into the mains and follows the instructions. Getting a new email address a source of amusement as he selects a suitable user name: NEDKELLY, CLYDEBARROW, ALCAPONE, ROBINHOOD....what to pick. He eventually selects   jimfiske@aol.com a choice he feels reflects his mood, the name being taken from Patrick Knowles character in *The Big Steal* from 1949.

He logs on and immediately goes to Google and types in Pilatus PC-12 and instantly a selection of pictures jump into view. He prints off some pictures and piles them up on the table. He then types in Shoreham Airport and does the same. Then a map of Hampshire, Dorset and one of Sussex. The research continues until he has a substantial pile of pictures printed and the ink cartridge flashes that it is running out. H stretches and looks at his watch and is amazed to find that it is 1am; he has been working solidly for twelve hours.

He strips and pulls on his pyjamas then a quick brush of his teeth and he climbs into bed. Sleep won't come though and he flicks on the light and sits making notes in his small book. Three or four pages of notes and his head slumps forward and he is asleep with his dreams of wealth and freedom.

CHAPTER SEVEN - GILBERT

The pale April morning sun warms H as he sits on an old wooden bench outside the confines of SummerVale, so lost in reverie that the soft tread of Buzz Lightyear slippers elude his earshot and he literally jumps as Gilbert says "Morning."

He comes around the bench and sits beside H.

"Jesus, you nearly gave me a heart attack."

Breathing heavily H looks down, closes his notebook then spots the bizarre footwear and looks at Gilbert.

"What *are* you wearing on your feet?"

"Slippers.......why."

""They're Buzz Bloody Lightyear slippers. A pair of the strangest looking Disneyfied fluffies I've ever seen. Fine for a six year old, not so for a sixty six year old dippy hippy."

H then adds "Unless he has the mental age of a six year old!"

H looks at the old man next to him, tatty maroon dressing gown, striped pyjama top, checked pyjama bottoms, the loud green action-figure slippers, white –grey pony tail and a skull and cross-bones bandana.

"What **do** you look like? If I had known you dressed like that I never would have talked to you. Is this standard attire for the mentally challenged now or are you the fashion guru that make all the others look so grey and worn out?"

Gilbert smiles, a spark of life burning back in his head that H had missed before.

"What have I got to get dolled up for? No-one comes to see me, no-one is gonna moan at me. Some days I don't get dressed at all. My life is drifting to a conclusion; I can get there in Buzz Lightyear slippers and a tatty dressing gown as easily as I could in a smart suit and hundred quid shoes. So sod 'em all."

"Sorry, I wasn't having a pop, just taking the piss a bit. I've been here a fortnight and I feel like I'm ready to shuffle off this mortal coil"

"No offence taken. Nearly everyone here is alone. Old people are an embarrassment to their families, they want them hidden away and causing no bother. The longer you remain here the more you will come to realise that old age is almost as socially unacceptable as looking like The Elephant Man."

"But you're still alive; George is firing on most cylinders, Gus is like a man of fifty, not nearly seventy. What keeps everyone so down?"

Gilbert strokes his wispy beard.

"They have all lost their spark. Like a lighter that can no longer ignite a flame, they have had the life beaten out of them, either mentally or in some cases physically. They are here as if it's the elephants' graveyard, they've come here to die."

"That's horrible. Are they all the same? What could make them wake up?"

"They have no reason to wake. Give them a reason and maybe they would respond. The majority of people here rarely think about the outside world now. It doesn't concern them. They can't afford real world luxuries; they don't want to be confronted by the realities of life outside this place so they make sure they aren't. It's a simple equation for them, no money equals no opportunities therefore keep life simple and they won't have to deal with reality."

H pulls a face.

"That's a load of bollocks."

Gilbert smiles. "Yeah, but it was more interesting than saying I've got no idea."

"Plonker."

H looks around; the quiet of their bench is still uninterrupted. He looks at Gilbert who has a curious openness about him, almost as if he's waiting for H to say something profound.

"What's your deal? Why are you stranded here and what do you want out of the remainder of your life?"

Gilbert tugs at his beard again.

"You're gonna pull that off if you keep tugging at it."

"I'm thinking."

H pulls at an imaginary beard on his face.

"Leave off. Ok, H, I've known you for just under two weeks and I've spoken more to you than I have to some people here that I've known for two years. Why is that? What's going on with you? Ok, I'll tell you. I had a really thriving design business. I had a great contract with my local co-op, the local authority and many local businesses. The co-op sold out to Asda, they didn't need me, and everything was done via Head Office. The local authority changed their officers and the contract went to another company doing it for half what I charged. My business started to fall apart, and so did I."

Gilbert lights a small cigarette, takes a long drag and picks a piece of tobacco from his lip and continues.

"I found out that my wife had run up some sizeable debts doing way too much retail therapy, she loved to shop. I hit the bottle and she decided the best way out of the mess we were in was to chuck herself under the 8.15 fast train to Northampton. I hit the bottle harder. The insurance company decided not to pay the life insurance as she had taken her own life and I had to sell everything to clear the debts. I didn't quite make it and was declared bankrupt, had no job, no home, no relatives and no prospects. The court took pity on me and placed me here in a subsidised deal. My state pension covers my extras, you know, food, tea, coffee and the occasional ciggie. They take care of the room and that's all there is."

The effort to tell his story has obviously affected Gilbert and he slumps back against the bench back. He takes a deep breath.

"So that's the deep story, I'm off the pop, not had a drink for three years, not much chance here anyway. So I crossed the river Styx and ended up here and here I remain."

"So what do you want to do with the rest of your days?"

"I have no idea. Who does? I do like to paint though. What do you want to do H?"

H, now more animated and keen to push Gilbert, leans closer to him.

"I want to be able to hold my head up again. I don't want to be left to rot here. I have a plan, or I may have a plan, very soon."

"Such as?"

"I want to rob the rich."

"Who are you….Robin Hood?"

"No, I don't intend to give any of the ill gotten gains to anyone, but keep them all to myself……..or ourselves."

Gilbert looks closely at H. "You're serious, what are you going to do?"

"Enough for now. More soon."

"H, you can't do that, tell me now."

H stands. He stretches his arms and flexes his legs.

"Let's walk."

H sets off across the gravel with Gilbert in hot pursuit.

The sloping lawn of the SummerVale grounds leads them away from the imposing house. H looks around to make sure they are out of earshot. Gilbert is alongside him, hands deep in his dressing gown pockets. He adopts a very poor Sean Connery accent:

"Ok Bond, whatsh the shtory."

H takes a deep breath, this has only just firmed up in his own mind and he hasn't really had time to formulate a proper presentation.

"When I was a barrister an old thief told me a story about a job he never pulled but always wanted to. I think we can do it."

"What me and you?"

"Well, we'll need more, lots more, to make it work."

Gilbert stops, spins H round by the shoulders.

"The living dead in there, robbing people. Most of them can't feed themselves and the others need to take a piss every 20 minutes. You're nuts."

"They cannot all have given up. Some of them still have some life in them. We just need to light the blue touch paper."

"They are old people not bloody Roman Candles."

H walks on, his head dropping a little, he is out of his comfort zone here and he is losing Gilbert.

"Listen, this is a chance to fight back, to show the world that life doesn't stop at 60. We can't get jobs, we can't get our lives back but we can do something to reclaim our self esteem. Just let me tell you the story and then tell me I'm nuts."

They have reached a wooden bench under a willow tree some 200 yards from the house. They sit and look back up the manicured lawn. H spots a small plaque screwed into the back of the seat. It is simple but poignant:

For Ernie – husband, rock, friend and redeemer. Miss you forever. Teresa.

"Do you want to end up as a plaque on a bench? Wouldn't it be nicer to lie on a beach in the Bahamas for the last years of your life?"

"Didn't do Ronnie Biggs any good did it?"

H starts to react but takes a breath.

"But they knew he had done the job, he was a fugitive on the run and it was Rio. I intend for us to be anonymous, unknown, and free."

Gilbert looks intently at H.

"Ok explain, I'm all ears."

So the two old men sit and talk on a quiet bench in a quiet corner of a Hampshire old folk's home and discuss taking the biggest gamble of their lives.

After twenty minutes of talking H sucks in a deep breath.

"Well, that's it. What do you think?"

"You're nuts. You *should* be locked up. You are off your trolley. Bonkersville."

"Fair enough, I just hate the thought of being a vegetable in this madhouse. I don't know any pilots but I'm sure I will find one."

Gilbert just stares at H. "Did you know Gus was a pilot?"

"How could I know that? Why would I know that? That's *very* interesting."

H looks out into the middle distance across the lawn, lost in thought.

"H, what are you thinking?"

"Huh?"

"Do you really think it's possible?"

H looks deep into Gilberts face.

"Oh yeah, it just needs some work, some organising and some bottle. Interested?"

"Maybe. Let me think about it."

H stands and looks back at SummerVale.

"What's tonight's entertainment?"

"Oh big time tonight my friend, Ronnie Gale and His Magic Organ playing a medley of Country and Western favourites."

"Oh joy unconfined. I'm going to get my spurs and wax my lasso."

"H, be careful, you could do yourself a mischief."

The two men chuckle as they make their way across the lawn.

H stretches his arms over his head as they walk.

"Only ten hours to kill before the fun starts."

"What a life eh? How do we escape this purgatory?"

They walk in silence with their own thoughts rattling around in their heads. H has just one phrase that won't go away.

"Wealth is freedom."

He shakes his head as they approach the entrance to SummerVale, he can see the residents queuing for their morning bran.

CHAPTER EIGHT - GUS

The idea of a night surrounded by wrinklies bopping to Bobby Crush on their Zimmer frames fills H with dread. The thought of a night with Ronnie Gale and his Limp Organ is almost unbearable, but, it's a chance for H to socialise a bit. He might have given up his time in the sun with work but he's not about to curl up and die completely. Besides, tonight he has an agenda. Gus. The nagging in the back of his brain won't go away; the idea is getting stronger each day. The more time he spends at SummerVale the more he is becoming determined to try it, at least to explore the idea, to see if Maurice actually knew what he was doing.

H puts on a black short sleeved shirt, black trousers and smart black suede loafers; he looks at his reflection in the mirror. No haunted eyes, no haggard face, he actually looks better than he has done for the last few months. In a very short space of time he has definitely taken a step toward looking a bit younger.

"Bizarre" he says to his image. He picks up a deep green carrier-bag lying on the bed and heads for the door.

H walks casually down the stairs, casually swinging his green bag from side to side.

He approaches the lounge door with some trepidation, opens the door a fraction and he is assaulted by a Muzak version of Dolly Parton's *Jolene* which is almost enough to send him running back upstairs, but a deep breath and in he goes.

Looking around the room he spies Gus sitting by the window overlooking the lawn. No chessboard in sight, no Gilbert in sight so he wanders over.

"Mind if I sit here."

"Sit thee down. This abominable noise is almost unbearable so a bit of company to distract me will be more than welcome. How are you settling into Colditz?"

H takes a seat next to Gus rather than opposite him.

"Not too bad thanks. A bit quiet."

H looks over at Ronnie Gale and his flashing organ.

"Except when **he's** in town."

Gus chuckles "Ain't that the truth."

H looks at Gus's glass, a small shot glass with dark brown liquid at the bottom, but not much. He opens the green carrier bag and removes a bottle with a ship on it, a bottle of Tortuga Rum, purchased at Oddbins that very afternoon. He raises the bottle to allow Gus to see. Gus' eyes light up.

"Ay oop my man, Tortuga Gold, angels milk. Amazing."

H unscrews the lid and pours Gus a generous measure. He pours himself a measure into a plastic glass that is one of four in the centre of the table.

They clink glasses and sip the dark fiery liquid.

Gus closes his eyes in ecstasy "Aaarrr, now that hits the spot."

H swallows a small amount and feels his throat burst into flames and he thinks his eyes might explode.

"Bloody Nora, that is powerful stuff."

Gus chuckles at H's reaction. Ronnie Gale starts to murder Hank Williams' – *Your Cheatin' Heart* and H thinks his eyes and his ears might explode.

Gus motions with his empty glass and H tops him up.

Gus takes a sip this time and looks closely at H.

"Very nice. But why?"

H leans in, takes a quick glance around, and no-one is taking a blind bit of notice of them as they all watch Ronnie strangle another Hank lyric.

"Gilbert told me you were from Antigua and liked a drop of rum, so a little research and Tortuga was the number one choice. I thought it might break the ice."

"That's lovely, I swear down this is the best drop I've tasted in many months. Thankee kindly."

"My pleasure Gus. So how come you're stuck here then?"

"Oh, circumstance and disaster. I made a few poor choices. How about you. Mister Lawyer man."

He looks at H as if to say 'I know stuff about you'.

H smiles.

"I have been turned over by my wife, she got the house, pension, savings. My kids got support payments and sided with their mother, work kicked me out and hired spotty replacements that are cheaper and useless; the system chewed me up and spat me out. After forty years of graft I have been dumped here to die."

Gus takes a sip of his rum, contemplates how much to tell this inquisitive new man, decides to share with him.

"Me too. I came over to England with me Mom and Da to Yorkshire in 1945. A dangerous place to arrive from Antigua. From empty golden beaches to muddy fields and driving rain. My Da worked down the pit, only time he wasn't different, everyone else had a black face then too." He smiles. "I used to bunk off school when I was about seven and go to watch the planes practice taking off and landing in open fields on the moors. Even though the war was over they kept practising just in case. Joined up in fifty seven, RAF apprentice. Trained as a pilot for nine years then spent twelve years flying all around the world. I always loved flying. I can fly anything tha' knows. Even had a go in one of them there hangliders once, like being suspended under a coat hanger strung with knicker elastic."

Gus takes a sip of rum. He is warming to his tale.

"I left the RAF in 1978 and spent some time travelling. Visited Antigua among other Caribbean Islands and then became a commercial pilot in 1980 and spent sixteen happy years flying through the skies in hundreds of different planes. Packed it in after a real dodgy flight to Pakistan in ninety six. Island hopped for a few years, made a massively stupid investment in 2002 and ended up here. The RAF pays for my room, Royal Air Force pension. Hmmmm. Still, it could be worse."

H slides another slug of rum into Gus' glass as the rumble of bad Country and Western goes on in the background.

Gus continues after a warming swig of Tortuga gold.

"I really felt the call of my roots, tha' knows. So I looked for a place to retire in Antigua. I found a lovely place, overlooking the sea, a view of Green Island, just off Nonsuch Bay. There is a place there called Curtain Bluff, the most beautiful place on this Gods earth. I put down a large deposit; it was a big, rambling house. The idea was that I could spend the rest of my days fishing and drinking rum."

Gus takes a large gulp of Tortuga special.

"But I still needed a big mortgage to cover the cost of the place and the money to do it up. I only ever rented in England so I needed to borrow to make up the difference so I put everything I had on the line. This little weasel stole every bean I owned and disappeared, the house wasn't even his to bloody sell. I really took a bath. My family disowned me and my ex-wife really ripped me apart, made my son turn against me, he's embarrassed that I won't be leaving him anything. He is a very angry young man. I'm just sad, and you know something H, there's no racial prejudice in sadness, it hits everyone the same. I hate the sameness of SummerVale; I loved travelling around the world. My time in the RAF was fantastic. My wife left me for another airman back in the eighties while I was doing shuttle runs to and from Italy. Bitch. So here I am, stuck in the heart of Hampshire with a group of dead people."

H pours the last of the rum into Gus' glass and they clink their plastic vessels together in silent acknowledgement of similar circumstances and they swallow their rum as Ronnie Gale tortures *Ring Of Fire* and a few old inmates clap along.

H decides to push the conversation forward.

"So Gus, what do you want from the rest of your life?"

"How do you mean?"

"Well, do you want to just stay here playing chess with Dylan from The Magic Roundabout or do you have a bigger goal? A dream?"

Gus looks long and hard at H. He plays with his empty plastic cup and replies.

"I would love to have my own place either in Yorkshire or, in an ideal world, a place by the sea in Curtain Bluff. Neither of those dreams is likely so I'll put up with my lot in life. I've even given up doing the lottery as it just made me anxious every Saturday and looking for the Barnsley result every Saturday is stressful enough."

H leaning ever closer.

"What would you say if I told you I might be able to offer you a chance to fulfil either of those dreams?"

"What's the catch? Who do I have to kill?"

"No one is going to be killed, but there will be a risk."

"Risk of what?"

H glances around.

"Prison."

Gus places the empty cup on the table and steeples his fingers in front of his face.

"An illegal act that might end up with a spell in prison. Prison, with no-one visiting me, not much different to here then."

Gus is totally unfazed.

"Not much risk really."

H is amazed at his calmness; he is sweating bullets under his shirt.

"Well, that's true I suppose, when you put it like that. Can you still fly?"

Gus sits upright.

"Of course. Well, I could, but not legally, without a licence. You have to renew each year. I haven't got a plane to fly so there was no reason to renew. Haven't had a licence for six years now. Could pass the eyesight test but I doubt if they would give me a licence now though. But why do you ask?"

H leans so close that they are touching shoulders.

"Ok, come to my room and I'll explain everything. Give me ten minutes."

H stands a little unsteadily as *Islands In The Stream* floats across the lounge to accompany him to the door. He realises the rum has affected him a lot more than he thought.

Back in number 68 H runs a basin of cold water and dunks his face in it to try and shake off some of the rum effect. As he emerges there is a knock at his door, drying his face he opens the door to Gus. He ushers him in, pokes his head around the door and checks an empty corridor and shuts the door behind them.

"Got no drinks to offer you I'm afraid. Cup of tea? Coffee?"

Gus shakes his head and plonks himself down in the only chair.

"No thanks, I'll be pissing like a racehorse as it is. I'm fine."

H picks up his folder and sits on the edge of the bed close to Gus.

"Ok, here's the deal. When I was defending an old thief he gave me the plans, very detailed plans of a robbery he never got to do. A daring, non violent plan to rob very rich people who want to smuggle their wealth out of the country to avoid paying inheritance tax or wealth tax or whatever."

Gus pushes his bottom lip out.

"I'm listening."

H continues.

"It involves flying a plane, our plane, into a small airport, loading a couple of crates and taking off again. Landing somewhere quiet and making off with the crates. No danger, no violence just a risk of imprisonment if we get caught."

"Oh well, let's do it then."

"Really?"

"No, not really you idiot. I thought you was a smart man. Mister lawyer man. Are you nuts? Have you thought this through? Where will you get a plane? How will you get away with it?"

H's eyes widen.

"Those are details. We're not there yet. I just want to find out if you are even vaguely interested. Would you take a chance to realise your dreams?"

Gus thinks about this statement for a moment.

"How much do you expect to get?"

"Now that's a better question."

H stands and walks back and forward by his small sink.

"Could be millions, could be a lot less but I think we'll be looking at one hundred thousand pounds each minimum.....tax free."

He lets this hang in the air. Gus whistles.

"That would buy me a small place in Antigua. What's the next step?"

H smiles, he's got his man.

"I'm going to do some more research and we'll make a list of requirements. But have a look at this."

He shows Gus the note from Maurice and the details. He sits back down and waits for Gus to read Maurice's scratchy handwriting.

"Well, your man did his homework but we need much more information. More detail."

"We will get it. For now are you interested?"

"Yes. Why not. We only get one life. I may as well end it in a jail cell as a lunatic asylum like this."

Gus laughs and holds out his hand. H shakes it firmly.

"We don't say anything to anyone until we're certain it will work. Ok?"

"No problem. I'm going to sleep off your rum."

Gus stands and heads for the door.

"See you in the morning."

"Have you got any pyjamas with arrows on them?"

H laughs as the door closes behind Gus. He lies back down on the bed and is still there as the first stirrings of morning rouse him from a rum fuelled sleep.

CHAPTER NINE – WILLY'S

H climbs into his Jaguar, now covered with a layer of dust. The bonnet and windshield speckled with the droppings of a hundred sparrows. He starts the engine and the thick tyres crunch slowly across the gravel. It's been just over a week since his drinking session with Gus and he has made plans as best he can in number 68 but now needs flesh on the bones of his idea. The early morning dew helps the windscreen wipers clear the dust and bird crap off the windscreen. Turning right out of the gates H is soon cruising along drumming his fingers to ZZ Top singing Sharp Dressed Man.

Dressed quite sharp himself in an old, but still stylish Paul Smith suit, open necked white shirt and suede black loafers he looks every inch the retired businessman, a look he wanted rather than an aged lawyer. On the seat next to him is Maurice's envelope and the key to lock box 319.

The M3 melts into the A3 and then more urban, local traffic, H's Jaguar makes slow progress as East London takes shape around him. As his destination gets closer H starts to fantasise "if I find a parking space straight away on the left hand side of the road then this will work."

Turning into Cordelia Street he sees a large dishevelled sign, neon bulbs exposed and the legend:

ILLY'S   ASH TERIA

H smiles at the lack of W's and an E then looks away and there, right beside him is an empty parking meter. He indicates left and pulls in, puts the Jag into park and switches off the engine. Looking at the meter there is maximum paid up time remaining. "Ok, that's a sign."

H picks up the key and the envelope, takes a huge breath and opens the door. He steps onto a relatively quiet street, swings the car door shut and locks it. He steps toward the building that might hold his destiny or might be his downfall.

Onto the pavement, three short steps to the open door. Peering inside he sees two women, one white, one black sitting in silence watching their smalls go round and round.

He steps over the threshold and walks straight into the biggest man he has ever seen. A huge beast in a lemon and gold shell suit open to the waist with a small collection of gold chains hanging among the thick black curls just level with his nose. The penny drops, this must be Costas. H swallows hard and looks up into a large, round face topped with curly black hair.

H smiles at this giant of Greek extraction, a weak somewhat frightened smile.

He enquires "Costas?"

The large face changes, his teeth disappear, eyes narrow and bushy eyebrows loom forward.

"Who wants to know?"

H swallows again.

"Maurice gave me this." Holding up the key and the envelope.

H, sweating a little continues

"Could we go somewhere ....to..err......talk?"

The man mountain softens his stance a little but still looks suspicious.

"Come through the back."

He turns on his heel and departs.

Very nimble for a big man H thinks and shakes his head for having such a bizarre thought jump into his head.

Avoiding the gaze of the two old biddies H follows the moving yellow mountain through a curtain of many coloured plastic strips and down a short corridor. He sees Costas step to the right and he follows.

They are in a room no larger than an average lounge except there is no furniture, no TV, no anything, just metal boxes set into the walls like safety deposit boxes floor to ceiling. H's eyes look around, up and down and are drawn to Box 319.

Costas steps in front of him, breaking his view of the box, and the rest of the room for that matter.

"So tell me how you know Mo?"

"Mo?"

"Maurice?"

"Oh yes."

"What's the score, he's been on the missing list for a while. Haven't seen him here for a few months now. Who are you and what do you want?"

H fumbles to open the envelope which feels quite damp from his sweaty palms.

"I was, am, well was, Maurice's barrister."

"Yeah?"

"I defended him many times over the years. I assume you know he spent some time in prison."

"Why would I know that?"

"I…well, that is….oh bugger."

The large face softens, he smiles at H.

"Yeah, I know Mo was a guest of her Maj's a few times. Chill."

H breaths a sigh of relief.

57

"After the last case a few weeks ago he retired and gave me this key and envelope and a letter detailing how to find Willy's and you. Although his description of a six foot seven bubble left me baffled until now."

Costas laughs out loud, a deep rumbling sound that threatens to make the walls shake. His huge Aegean features much more agreeable than when he's scowling.

"Cheeky old sod. So he's really retiring, out of the game. Good on him."

H looks quizzically at Costas, does he know more than he's letting on?

"Erm, Maurice said you would need a hundred pounds to close off his account on the lock box."

Reaching into his pocket H gives the Goliath the envelope. Costas tucks it into the pocket of his bulging shell suit and zips it up. No opening it or counting the contents.

Who would cross this guy anyway H thinks.

Costas moves to the left and gestures to Box 319. H moves in mumbling a thank you. He inserts the key into the lock and turns it, a loud click and the door swings open easily. Inside the lock box a tin box contains a cardboard box that H lifts out. He turns the key to the now empty box 319 and hands it to Costas without a word. He tucks the box under his arm and stands back.

Costas motions to the way out and they reverse the way they came in until they are back in the launderette. The two old ladies are still sitting in the same spot watching the washing spin. They walk to the door in silence.

At the door Costas puts a giant paw on H's shoulder. He jumps and his heart starts to race. What next?

Costas leans down and has his head close to H's shoulder.

"Mo says hello and good luck."

H spins and looks at Costas smiling face.

"You've spoken to him? You knew who I was? You knew I was coming? How?"

"So many questions man. He just mentioned you might be along and that it was ok. Told me to be gentle with you. Said you were ok. Like old Mo. Lovely fella. You take care now. You know where I am if you need anything Mr H."

Bewildered, H says one last weak thank you and walks to the Jaguar. As he opens the door Costas calls from the doorway he's totally blocking.

"Nice wheels."

And with that he's gone from H's view.

H gets in, places the box on the passenger seat and looks at his hands. They are shaking wildly.

"Christ I've got Parkinsons." Then looks around as he has said this out loud.

Cruising back down the M3 he can't help staring at the box on the seat next to him. He had decided not to open the box (unless forced to) until he was back in the safety of his room at . SummerVale and he is determined to stick to his plan. The pull of the contents is massive like some Indiana Jones treasure. He places his hand on the lid and drums his fingers as he hums along to Wreckless Eric singing *Whole Wide World*.

Turning into SummerVale he smiles as he sees the artwork by the old boy he now refers to as Banksy is still in place.

"Home Sweet Home."

He parks under the sparrow toilet and locks the car. He walks to the door and surveys the quiet view of the lawn. Glancing at his watch he knows the main room will be full of munching geriatrics, it being lunchtime. He is too excited to eat so he hurries up the stairs to his room, shuts the door and pulls his chair up to the door to prevent unwanted entrants.

He sits on the edge of the bed and puts the cardboard box on his lap. He wipes his sweating hands on the duvet and lifts the lid.

CHAPTER TEN - MEETING

His getting dressed, the contents of Maurice's box scattered over the bed and every available surface of number 68. Maps, photos, lots of photos, schedules, pictures of planes, scribbled sheets of notes, the culmination of years of research by Maurice. Most amazingly there is a brick of used notes, possibly three thousand pounds H thinks.

As H pulls on his sweater he catches sight of himself in the mirror, he looks relaxed and as focussed as if he was in charge of a major case. Having set up a meeting in the garden with Gus, Gilbert and George he needs to have all his ducks in a row. Almost all night he has been making notes in a little black notebook, separate pages for every participant. He packs away the photos, sheets of paper and then hides the box under his bed. He picks up his notebook and folder, and heads for the door.

Outside in the morning sunshine H turns away from SummerVale and heads across the lawn, past the neat clipped borders and into the sheltered area over 100 yards from sight. As he turns into a hedge trimmed square he sees the three men sitting on a wooden bench.

H smiles at them, they all look serious.

"See no evil, hear no evil, think no evil."

Gus smiles back.

"More like Groucho, Chico, Harpo."

George chips in.

"Larry, Moe and Curly."

Both men look at Gilbert for any offerings from him.

He raises his eyes and joins the debate.

"The Good, The Bad and The Ugly."

H chuckles.

"Bacon, lettuce and tomato."

Gus points his finger at each of them.

"There are four of us, The Four Musketeers?"

Gilbert nods and adds.

"Sex, drugs, rock and roll."

H is happy that they are all smiling, he takes control.

"Ok guys, not sure which is which but I'll settle for roll. Now, we all know why we're here. I have an idea, a chance for us all to get out of here and have a real life for the rest of our days. This is a bit dangerous, definitely illegal and potentially lucrative. I know Gus and Gilbert are in, George you had a chance to think about it?"

George turns the sides of his mouth down and nods.

"If you three think it can be done then I'm in. What's the story H?"

H sits on the armrest of the bench.

"Great. Here's the deal."

He opens the folder.

"Every month a small plane, a Pilatus PC-12...."

H removes a photo of the plane that was in Maurice's box and hands it to Gus and continues.

"...lands at Shoreham airport and loads two or three large crates. Here's a long shot photo of the crates, bit distant but you can see the size."

He hands the photo to George,

"They are filled with lockboxes, metal cases and the like filled with cash, jewels and money the rich and famous want to hide from the tax man. It's not insured as its illegal and they won't call the cops for the same reason."

Gus waves the photo of the plane.

"This is a nice little plane. Not too common. I have some questions?"

H stops him.

"All in good time, let me outline the whole situation then we can go through all your questions."

"Ok."

H carries on; he has rehearsed his speech, the layout and timing of his presentation.

"So, the idea is to buy the exact same plane. Paint it with the same numbers, markings etcetera and then delay the proper flight, land our plane in its place, load the crates and take off again but we won't be off to Switzerland. We will land in a field nearby, unload the crates and disappear."

The other three men are silent, so H continues.

"I will do a recce of the airport soon. I intend to watch the airport on the last Thursday of this month then we do the job the following month."

H hands a picture of the airport to Gilbert and the men look at it. They swap the photos H has handed out and take a moment to digest all H has said.

H carries on.

"The contents of the cases will be distributed equally among all those who take part. I think we could be looking at one hundred K each."

George whistles through his teeth and the others nod in sage agreement.

"There are a load of other details but let's go through your questions. Gus?"

Gus takes the picture of the plane back from Gilbert.

"The plane. Where do we get it?"

H responds.

"We buy one. A second hand one. We buy the special airplane paint and make it the same as the plane due in."

"What with?"

This comes from all three men together.

"We pool all our resources. Anyone putting money in gets a full share."

Gus shakes his head.

"You don't understand, buying a second hand plane is not like picking up an old Astra you don't get Arthur Daley with a plane lot in every town."

"Well I didn't think that was the case but we'll have a lot of homework to do and some money to find."

"Ok, let's suppose we get all the info we need on the plane and we get the money and we buy the plane. Where do we find the details of the flight and where do we get a licence for me to fly the plane, I'm assuming you want me to fly the plane?"

H takes a typed A4 sheet from his folder and hands it to Gus. It contains flight times, flight numbers and names. He nods his head at Gus.

"Absolutely."

Gus glances at the sheet. George and Gilbert glance over. George smiles and in a faintly sarcastic voice says.

"Oh yes, I see what all that means."

Gus nods.

"Course you do, Lindbergh."

Gus waves the piece of paper at H.

"Ok, so we have the details, the times and possibly the plane. How do we get the proper plane to be delayed?"

H refers to his little black book.

"I have an idea about that. We'll send a couple to Switzerland and book them on the flight, the old guy then fakes a heart attack, he's old and it will be believable, the plane is then forced to land at the nearest airport. We then say its ok we are coming in as the old guy is alright and we land, load the crates and leave."

The three old pals nod.

George leans forward.

"Who can we get to fly to Switzerland and get on the plane?"

Gilbert raises his finger.

"What about getting Trisha on board and maybe Ernie as her husband, he gets on as well as anyone with Trisha."

"That could work." George is warming to the theme now.

H makes a note in his book.

"I'll have a word with her and Ernie. They will need passports and some new clothes. We are getting somewhere now. Gus to fly the plane, Trisha and Ernie to delay the real plane, us three to unload the crates and hide the plane after we do the job."

Gus grins.

"So I'm flying a plane we don't have, using a pilot's licence I don't have and land at an airport we don't have paperwork to visit hoping the real plane is delayed by two people who don't yet know about the job, loading crates containing stuff we don't know anything about then take off again and land in a field, unload the crates and escape while not being spotted by anyone!"

H smiles at Gus.

"That's about the size of it."

George puts his hands up in a gesture of understanding

"Well that's ok then."

H decides to press on.

"So, we need to know what our next jobs are."

The three men hunch closer. H continues.

"Gus, we need a contact or company to buy a plane from, I'll need your old pilot's licence so I can obtain a new one and a passport photo. Gilbert, I need you to check out a large van, white, indistinguishable from all the other white vans we see on the road. George, you're with me on the trail of Trisha and Ernie, and I'll need your keyboard expertise at a later date, but we can work on that. Ok?"

The three old guys nod.

"Right, let's get to work. Meet again on Tuesday, here, same time, that gives us two days to find what we need. Alright."

"Yes."

"Yep."

"Yeah man."

The four musketeers stand and head back to SummerVale, a definite spring in their step as they head for a bite of breakfast before starting their tasks.

CHAPTER ELEVEN - TRISHA

Walking into the breakfast arena, H and George side by side, Gus and Gilbert behind them they cut a strange sight, a quartet of smiling old men with their own little secret.

Gus and Gilbert take their customary seats and begin to lay out their chess pieces. A wheeze behind them and the scrape of a Zimmer frame and Fred James comes up to the table.

"Wondered if you was coming? You're late, where have you been?"

Gus puts the last white pawn into place.

"Mind your own business."

"I only asked, you've never been late before, just wondered what kept you."

Gilbert picks up a black and a white pawn and puts them in his hands under the table.

"We've been smoking a spliff round the back."

Fred is getting annoyed that they won't tell him anything.

"Sod off hippy."

Gus looks at Gilbert.

"Left."

Gilbert reveals the white pawn in his left hand.

"Your start."

He replaces the two pawns and settles back to see where Gus moves.

Gus eases a white pawn out two places in front of his bishop.

"You are a charming old fart Fred. Leave us to our game."

Fred is dismissed but leaves slowly; he walks past Gus and leans closer.

"By the way Gus, you play chess like Stevie Wonder."

Gus laughs as Gilbert finishes his move.

"I've seen you on that Zimmer frame Fred, and let me tell you, you drive it like Ray Charles. Bog off"

Meanwhile H and George have taken some cereal and taken seats at a table close to Trisha and Margaret. H takes a mouthful of cornflakes and surreptitiously glances across at the two women. He realises that underneath the shabby dress and straggly hair Trisha is still a handsome woman. Life may have beaten her down but she still has something. He puts his spoon down and looks at George.

"Cup of tea George."

"No thanks. I'm fine."

"Are you sure George?"

He stresses his future partner in crime's name.

George looks up and realises H is up to something.

"Oh ok, go on then, four sugars."

H shakes his head in disbelief. He stands and walks past the two women close by.

He smiles as he goes past.

"Morning ladies."

They both look up. Margaret smiles but Trisha looks as if she is sucking a lemon.

"Can I get you a tea or coffee? I've got to get George a sugar rush cuppa, would you like one?"

Margaret looks at Trisha almost for approval.

"That would be very nice, thank you, one sugar."

Looking at Trisha

"And you my dear?"

"No sugar and I'm not."

"Not what?"

"Your dear."

"Fair enough, back in a moment."

H walks off puffing his cheeks out.

He returns quickly with two cups.

"One sugar for you." Putting a cup in front of Margaret.

"And no sugar for you as you're sweet enough."

Trisha looks up, daggers in her eyes thinking H is being a little sarcastic. She sees that he is smiling and despite herself, she smiles back.

H turns and gets two teas for himself and George. He walks back to their table and puts a cup in front of George.

"One cup of sugar with some tea in it."

"Blimey H, what did you say? She smiled for Gods sake!"

"See, there's life in all of us."

H takes a sip of his tea and nearly chokes.

"Oh my God." He splutters loudly and looks at the two ladies.

"That's his cup of syrup. Yuk."

They both laugh at H's reaction to the sugary tea.

He switches the two cups and winks at George. He knew what he was doing; he knew he had to make them laugh.

George sips his sweet tea.

"Nice one H."

They sip their tea in silence for a few minutes. Every now and again H looks over at the ladies table and smiles. The third time, he catches Trisha's eye and she smiles back.

H waits on his own drinking tea until Margaret leaves for a wee. He moves in to talk to Trisha (he is nearly bursting his bladder after drinking so much tea but might not have much time).

He sits down opposite Trisha. George stands behind him and moves to a table by the window. H leans forward.

"Hello, my name's….." Before he can finish Trisha interrupts.

"That's Margaret's seat. She'll be back."

"I know, just wanted to say hello."

"Why?"

"Well, we're all here together; I've been here a few weeks now and hardly know anyone."

Trisha hasn't stopped knitting for even a second.

"You talk to the three de - G's."

H realises she means Gus, Gilbert and George and laughs at the 70's girl band reference. He joins in the humour by almost singing:

"When will they see you again. Who named them that?"

Trisha smiles. A lovely smile in a very sad face.

"Oh, there is still a spark of humour in some of us old biddies here."

"I think there's more to this place than meets the eye."

The clacking needles continue.

"You're Alan Hitchcock."

"Call me H."

Trisha smiles again

"Hello H."

She stresses the first letter rather than saying Aitch. H finds this endearing.

"I'm Trisha."

"I know, George told me."

"Did he now."

She stops knitting and looks deep into his face.

"So what brings a man like you, educated, refined." She pauses. "Handsome and not really the type we are used to, into a place like this."

"What, do I smell?"

"No, you don't dribble."

H smiles.

"Well, it's a long story and I'm sure you've heard it all before. Wife, kids, work, life, government, all turn you over and you end up here. You can curl up and die or you can find that spark to keep you alive."

Trisha looks over his shoulder, is she looking to end the conversation or ensure it carries on. He's not sure.

"And have you?"

"Have I what?"

"Found that spark."

H smiles again.

"Maybe."

Trisha takes her teacup and has a sip. H continues.

"So what's a nice old girl like you doing in a place like this?"

The smile on H's face tells her he's being humorous with the 'old' comment so she continues.

"Well, it's like this, you know the saying – a fool and his money are soon parted."

H nods.

"It works as – a fool and **her** money too. My first husband, Pierre, died of cancer."

"Sorry."

"It was a long time ago. Easy how the time slips by. I lived in France you know, Paris first then a beautiful village just near Carcassonne called Montolieu, a small town dedicated to books. My husband was a writer, a novelist; we had a wonderful house with a quaint garden. The house was used by the resistance in the war; they even held meetings in the basement while the Nazis were dining in the rooms above."

Trisha pauses, lost in a suddenly painful memory.

"Pierre got sick, we went back to Paris, he had cancer, and he died. I had a few years alone then got my head stuck in a dream, a dream that love can conquer all. That a fit young healthy man would really fall for a middle aged frumpy grey, sad woman. I dreamed, he dropped me and cleaned me out. I didn't see it coming. Took me almost ten years to come to terms with it. I've been here seven years now and I think you are the first man I've been civil to. Why is that?"

H smiles once again.

"Because I'm a great listener, a smart dresser and a sucker for a woman who knits."

Trisha unconsciously touches her messy hair.

"No, it's because no-one has given a shit about talking to me for years. No-one cares what happens to us in here. We're out of sight, out of mind and if we keep ourselves clean and tidy and quiet then we can slide away to a timely end with no fuss. Great reward for sixty years of living. But you seem to have a much different view on life here and that has intrigued me more than anything in a very long time. Why do you and the Three-de-G's keep such close counsel these days? "

H edges forward and prepares to carry on when a presence behind him makes him stop. He looks over his shoulder and Margaret is standing glaring at him. He stands and offers her chair back.

"Here you go Mags. Park your bum."

Margaret spits back.

"My name is Margaret and please don't talk about my bu… bot…person, thank you."

She sits and H smiles his goodbyes and leaves. As he goes he turns and smiles at Trisha who is still looking at him. He pulls a weird face and she laughs. Margaret spins round and he looks away.

H walks on. He looks back and holds up seven fingers so Trisha can see. He gestures with his fingers and mouths 'here'. Trisha nods and H spins away.

He walks to where George is sitting by the window and leans down.

"If I don't get to the loo in the next thirty seconds I'm going to have an accident, back in a minute."

H waddles off to the loo.

At seven o'clock, H is sitting in a quiet corner of the lounge when Trisha enters. She has brushed her hair and smartened herself up, she looks ten years younger just with a few small changes. She looks around, catches sight of him and walks over. H stands as she approaches and motions to the other chair.

Trisha smiles and sits.

"Very gallant."

"Just manners, my Mum said they cost nothing but say everything."

"Clever woman."

"Not really, just a decent old soul with a good heart. Never did a bad thing in her life."

Trisha settles back in her seat, relaxed.

"What became of her?"

"She got pneumonia and died aged eighty, just a few years ago. The witch had taken all my money by then and I couldn't help my Mum. I suppose that's when I became bitter and twisted. Still, all a while ago now."

Trisha shocks H by leaning over and pats his hand. A gentle gesture but one that speaks volumes.

"You look fabulous by the way."

Trisha touches her hair.

"Thank you. Thought I'd smarten myself up a bit."

She looks thoughtfully at H.

"So, what are you and the three unwise men up to? You walk around chatting and then they all suddenly have a bit more spring in their step. They no longer sit around in their pyjamas all day. What have you done to them? Have you found the hippy some of that funny tobacco? Gus hasn't smiled this much in all the time he's been here. Why?"

"Well, it's a long story but I have a plan to make them all richer and more independent than they've been in their life."

"Winning the lottery is a long shot."

"It's a bit more involved than scratch and sniff cards. I want to steal a couple of crates from an airport. The proceeds will be split evenly among all those involved."

Trisha looks as if someone has slapped her round the face.

"Are you mad? They lock people up for stealing you know."

"I know, except, the stuff we are stealing is rich people's ill-gotten gains they are trying to hide. They can't call the police as they would have awkward questions to answer."

"So how do you expect to pull off this robbery?"

H takes a deep breath and tells Trisha the plan. He talks constantly for ten minutes without interruption until his story is over. Trisha looks at him for a long moment.

"You are madder than poor Mavis and she keeps a mouse in her knickers in the winter so it won't get cold. You are old men, worn out old men. Why do men think they can do the things they dreamed about in their youth? And more to the point, why have you told me all this?"

"Because I need your help."

"How?"

"Well, the plane I told you about does a shuttle service from Lugano Airport and lands and loads up the cargo in twenty to thirty minutes. We need to stop the real plane and land ours. I want you and a fellow volunteer to board the plane in Switzerland then fake illness forcing it to land at another airport early then we fly in, land and load the crates and fly off to a location here in the UK, land, unload the stuff, hide the plane and disappear."

Trisha is sitting with her mouth open. H reaches across and pushes her lower jaw up to close her mouth.

"Well, that's what we've been discussing. If it's not for you I'm sorry. When the money harpie took everything I had and my meagre pension was Maxwelled I realised the only way to get through my remaining years was to fight back. This is me fighting back. "

"But what if we get caught?"

H realises she included herself in this statement, using *we* rather than *you!* He smiles, this is a smart woman, a woman with guts too.

"Who's going to believe a bunch of old farts like us would even dream about doing something like this. And anyway, you won't do anything wrong. Just taking a flight from Switzerland is not illegal. Being ill on a plane is not illegal. We boys will be doing the only illegal thing. You wouldn't ever get convicted on the evidence available even if we get caught."

"Boys?"

"Well………..old boys then."

"More like it. But prison at my age would not be easy. I want open space and freedom."

"You would not be locked up; no-one is going to press charges, that's the beauty of this caper."

"Caper? Is this a movie?"

"Not yet. And let's hope not."

"Why not?"

"'Cos if it was, it would mean we got caught."

"Oh, good thinking. Maybe keep it a secret then."

"So, you interested?"

Trisha looks out of the window for a long moment. She takes a deep breath.

"I am sixty three years old. I have had a safe life and then a reckless life that destroyed the chance of a comfortable old age. I've never done anything dangerous….until now. Yes, I'm in, tell me more."

H smiles. He is more pleased with her saying yes than he thought he should be.

"Terrific."

H stands and looks down at Trisha.

"I have some more work to do. Can we have a meet in the morning?"

"I'll be here. Got nowhere else to go" She pauses and smiles up at H.

"Yet."

"Perfect, see you then. Oh, one last thing.....you'll need to pick someone to travel as your husband. Bye."

Trisha smiles back at H.

"Bye."

H walks out of the lounge and heads for the stairs. He has work to do.

CHAPTER TWELVE - THE HOOK

H looks at his watch, 7.15am. He realises he has been up all night again, working on the detail of the plan. Strangely he feels wide awake and not at all tired.

He decides to have a quick wash and get his ducks in a row for the morning meeting with Trisha and a later get together with Gus, George and Gilbert. A swift squirt of deodorant and a change of clothes and he is ready to present the next step.

He takes four manila folders from the bottom of his sock drawer and carefully places them side by side on his bed – still carefully made as he has not disturbed the sheets through the night.

He opens his wardrobe and takes out a map of Europe and carefully unfurls it. Sliding open another drawer he removes a packet of blu-tac and picks off four small pieces and uses them to stick the map on the wall by his bed.

He goes back to the wardrobe and removes a large piece of white card and follows the same procedure attaching this to the wall as well but uses eight pieces of blu-tac. The white card is covered with a dozen photographs all carefully taped at the sides by cello tape and H has written something beneath each picture.

Lastly H takes an A4 pad from the top of his chest of drawers and he places it on his chair. He is ready.

At 9.00am there is a firm rap on the door and on opening it H is confronted by Gus, Gilbert, George and Trisha all poised to enter. H steps aside and they all walk quickly into the room.

H settles the four of them on the bed next to the manila folders, each with their name on one. They all sit next to their own named folder without H having to say a word. H stands in front of them and picks up the A4 pad from his chair.

"Morning."

In unison they all reply. "Morning."

H sits, then stands, then sits again. He is nervous, this is a make or break moment for his plan.

He continues.

"Right then. We have all had a chat about this idea of mine to change our lives for the better. I have prepared a folder for each of you but if you can hold off looking inside it will help what I have to say."

Gus and Gilbert put down their folders like two naughty schoolboys caught eating sweets.

H licks his lips and continues.

"As you know the idea is to intercept the cargo of a plane that is to land at Shoreham Airport. The way we are going to do that is really very simple. We will buy our own plane, paint it the same colour as the real plane and also add the correct identification registration."

Gus half raises his hand and asks.

"How will we know that registration? Every plane has a unique serial number."

H puts his pad down and pulls a mobile phone from his pocket and waves it at them.

"With one of these. Trisha will be in Switzerland at Lugano Airport and as soon as she sees the plane she texts or calls us and we will be ready with the paint."

Seeing no real fault in the plan Gus just nods.

H places the phone back in his pocket and picks up his note pad again.

"So, we have established what we want to do. Now, how do we do it?"

H walks around the bed gently stepping carefully over the slipper clad toes of Gus and Gilbert until he is standing by the map of Europe.

A red cross marks Lugano Airport and a blue cross marks Shoreham Airport. H points at the red cross.

"Lugano Airport, Switzerland. Home to dodgy banks and dodgier bankers. The rich and famous use this place to hide their wealth from the tax man. The route to take their goodies away bizarrely starts and ends here but goes via Shoreham."

He moves his finger to the small cross on the south coast of England.

"The plane we seek will take off..." H consults his pad..." at nine am Swiss time. That's ten am our time. It will land normally at twelve twenty our time. We have to delay the proper plane by a couple of hours. That's where Trisha comes in."

H looks at Trisha.

"You can open your file Trish."

She likes his familiar use of her name, she smiles inside. She opens her file. Inside is a Timetable for a private airline, an on-line generated picture of Lugano Airport, detailed timings of trains and buses, a photo shop picture of the inside of a Pilatus PC-12. Trisha removes these one by one. Gus looks over her shoulder and hums his approval at the sight of the classy looking little plane. Trisha raises her shoulder as if Gus is cheating at a school exam.

H carries on.

"The idea is for Trisha and a man posing as her husband, partner, friend, whatever, will board the plane at Lugano and twenty minutes after take-off he will have a heart attack – not a real one, but a good fake one – and the plane will be forced to land somewhere quickly so he can get treatment. This will buy us at least the two hours we need to load the cargo and get the hell out of Dodge before the alarm bells ring."

H looks at the three men, then at Trisha.

No-one says a word.

"Any questions?"

Trisha glances at the pictures and the timetables. She looks back up at H.

"Who is this man going to be?"

"Well, we've got to decide that. Can we wait until I'm finished?"

They all nod their agreement.

H points at the large white card with the photographs attached. The other four turn then stand to see the pictures better. H points at the first picture on the top left of the card. It is a close up of the plane in Trisha's folder.

"A Pilatus PC-12. Nice plane. Very sleek." Enthuses Gus.

"Correct. This is the plane that ferries cargo to Switzerland to avoid the owners paying tax. And this…"

H moves to the second photo.

"is the sort of crates they load up every trip."

The photo shows two very large wooden crates on the tarmac beside the small plane.

H moves his finger along to another shot of the crates being loaded by a small forklift truck.

The next photo is of the inside of an airport.

"Lugano, small airport in Switzerland. This is where the goods are offloaded. The crates are fast-tracked through there and end up here…"

Once again he moves along and points to a photo; it's the front of a bank.

"This is Hetlinger and Cie, the bank that likes to say a great big bloody yes! The crates are delivered by armoured truck to this branch in Lugano and the contents are never seen again."

George lifts his reading glasses and stands very close to the photo.

"Is that an armed guard on the door?"

"Don't worry; we're never going near the place."

"I know that, just interested in how seriously they take security."

"Let's not worry about that just yet. The crates end up here but start at Shoreham Airport."

Next row down, a small, rural airfield, lots of little planes. A row of three photos show little or no people in any of the pictures.

"Is that tumbleweed in the distance?" Gilbert enquires.

"Quiet as any airfield in the South of England according to my notes." H moves on.

The final picture in the middle row shows a pilot in uniform. H looks at it.

"Gus, you'll look great in that uniform."

"He'll look like Tom Cruise in Top Gun." Trisha observes.

"More like Morgan Freeman in Driving Miss Daisy." chuckles Gilbert then dodges an arm flashing out to thump him.

H moves to the bottom row of photos and the first one shows a large field. It is fairly flat, trees on either side and a large barn at the far end. The second photo is the same field from the reverse angle, the third is a closer shot of the barn, it is huge and has two very large doors at the front and the last photo is from inside the barn, it is vast, sun streaming through cracks and missing boards and completely empty.

"This is where we will hide our plane and unload the crates. We will have a car and crow bars and hammers and stuff all waiting here and provided Gus thinks he can land in this field we've got a plan."

H is clearly worn out from this presentation but his audience have only just begun. Gus, Gilbert, Trisha and George all start asking questions at once.

"Whoa. One at a time."

H points at Gus.

"Gus, you go first."

"Ok. The field looks fine. I can land there no problem. Taxiing to the barn, no problem."

"Excellent."

"But how do we get clearance to land our plane and load the cargo, it'll be in the flight manifesto, how will we get that?"

H puts his arm on George's shoulder.

"That's where my hacking, racking and stacking pal comes in. George is going to hack into their computer, download the flight manifesto and re – route any other planes for that same landing time. We will have access to all the information in plenty of time to prepare."

Trisha looks amazed.

"You can do that?"

George shrugs.

"It's easy. Any system that's been built by a man can be unbuilt by a man, if you follow my drift."

Impressed, Trisha grins and looks differently at George.

"Well Bill Gates eat my dust."

H pulls the meeting back in line.

"So, we have the flight details, Gus is uniformed up and the real plane is delayed. We land, load the gear, take off and land in the field. Unload the crates, load the car and skedaddle as quickly as possible."

The four inmates look up at H and once again all start talking at once.

"Gus, you first."

"I will need a pilot's licence, just in case we get sent to a checking area. A passport to back it up and flight manifesto papers."

H makes notes on his pad.

"Ok. Trisha?"

"I'm going to Switzerland to board this plane with an as yet unspecified man as my partner. I …we, board the plane with legal tickets?"

"Yes."

"Then twenty minutes into the flight he fakes a heart attack and we hope the plane will emergency land somewhere like France to get him help."

"That's right."

"And what if they don't land early?"

"They will, its policy."

"Oh, ok then."

"Good, George?"

"Well, to crack the Airport system I'll need a couple of hours alone, with lots of quiet, shouldn't be too difficult."

"Great, Gilbert?"

"What's my function?"

"I need you to help me get the car or maybe a van, then drive it to the barn, we'll need to paint a new registration on our plane so it marries up with their log. You'll need to help us unload the goods and lock everything away. Lots of graft."

"But a big reward. Cool."

H is pacing around the room, he is animated, excited, vibrant, a man in full flow.

"Right, I'll sort Gus' licence and passport, I'll get Trisha a new one, pick a name, I have the cash for that. We need a partner for Trisha though."

Silence around the room as they all try to think who will fit into their little 'firm'.

Trisha smiles.

"Margaret."

Collectively they exclaim.

"What?"

"No listen, we will be two aging lesbians, the world is so PC they would never question us. Fear of reprisals from the sensible - shoes brigade."

H is impressed.

"Brilliant. But will she do it?"

"I'll talk her into it, leave that with me."

"She seems so frail. Is she up to it?"

Trisha nods her head.

"Yes, I think so, she needs a cause and this will bring out the best in her."

H is waving his hands around and the room is full of energy. The five of them are all stony faced in their determination.

H decides that they have gone far enough for one early morning. He starts to take down the map and they all realise the meeting is over. The white card is replaced in the wardrobe along with the map. Gus, Gilbert, George and Trisha pick up their folders and look expectantly at H.

He realises that they don't know whether to keep them or not.

"Take them with you, but keep them somewhere safe. On their own they mean nothing but collectively they would put us in deep poo."

Trisha hugs hers close to her chest, Gilbert slides his into the back of his trousers, Gus puts his military style under his arm and George holds his calmly by his side.

H smiles at them.

"Anyone for breakfast?"

They all file out of H's room and head downstairs.

CHAPTER THIRTEEN - COSTAS

As H turns the corner of Cordelia Street he feels a rise of panic in his chest. This is a whole different ballgame. His phone call to Costas the day before had gone well. He felt he had conveyed what he wanted to discuss without actually saying anything. They had set the meeting for mid-morning and H had set off from SummerVale at eight to make sure he was not late. He finds a parking space once again, close to the washeteria.

He fills the meter and strides to the door of Willy's Washeteria. As he walks through the door the same two old ladies are sitting in the same seats. He thinks they must be employees; no-one would come here unless they have a reason.

He steps cautiously toward the back of the ancient launderette and suddenly the light is blocked out as Costas appears, a vision in a turquoise shell suit.

A huge dark haired paw is extended and Costas growls.

"Come on through Mr H."

H shakes his hand, a child's palm in King Kong's fist. He goes through the multi coloured plastic strands and walks down the narrow corridor, once again wondering how on earth the behemoth behind him manages to fit in such a small space.

"Turn left, into the kitchen."

H does as he is instructed and finds himself in a small kitchen with a couple of chairs either side of a plastic covered table. Costas motions for H to sit, he complies.

Costas lowers his huge bulk onto the other chair and H wonders if it will hold, mentally deciding that the designer and manufacturer should get some sort of design award.

"So Mr H, what can I do for you?"

H takes a deep breath and decides to dive in.

"When I was here last you said if I needed anything to just ask. So, I need a pilot's licence and three passports. Can you help?"

H exhales and breaths hard through his nose trying to control his heart rate.

Costas looks long and hard at H. Then he smiles.

"Possibly. It's not cheap and it's illegal."

H understands that Costas needs to know that he's not being set up. He realises that he is being asked to confirm that he's not setting him up.

"Costas, old Maurice spoke very highly of you and in the stuff he left me he suggested I might use you if I needed anything to help with a job. I know the items I asked about are illegal; I need these things for an illegal act. You will not be involved or implicated and nothing will ever lead back here. It's all on me. If you can't help then that's fine. No harm no foul. I just don't have anywhere else to start."

Costas is smiling. He is happy that H has opened up enough to ensure that any arrest would now be entrapment.

"Sorry Mr H, gotta be careful."

"That's ok. I understand."

"Well, I'll need photos, age details, and a suitable address for the passports. They cost five hundred each. The pilot's licence will also be five hundred and I'll need a copy to show someone."

H reaches into his jacket pocket and removes an A4 sheet with all relevant details and Gus' old pilot's licence. There is also a small white envelope with passport size photos.

"The names are on the back of the photos."

He reaches into his other pocket. He removes a bulging wad of notes, the one Maurice left him. He puts the wad on the table.

"Here's two grand. Is that ok?"

Costas puts the money on the side of the table.

"That'll do nicely."

H leans back in his chair.

"When do you need them?"

H licks his lips.

"Two weeks? Is that possible."

"Not a problem. Come back in twelve days and I'll make sure they are ready."

H realises that the meeting is over. He stands and looks at Costas, now almost at his eye-line because he is still sitting. H extends he hand.

Costas takes it in his mighty grip.

"You be careful Mr H."

"Thanks Costas, I will."

H walks down the corridor and through the plastic drapes. Out through the launderette past the still chatting old ladies and back to the safety of his comfy old jag.

Sitting in the front seat he realises that he is sweating profusely. He leans back in his seat and clenches his fists and closes his eyes. Now things are really taking shape. Turning the key in the ignition he hears *Talking Heads – Road To Nowhere* flooding into the car.

H grips the wheel and out loud says

"Oh no, we're on the road to somewhere David."

He pulls out of his parking space and sets off back to SummerVale. Once out of the main traffic he pulls over and makes a note in his diary for twelve days time. It simply says "passports".

He makes a quick phone call to Gus and arranges to meet later in the day to de-brief.

H has one last call to make and drops in at a car-phone warehouse and buys six disposable mobile phones, all pay-as-you-go. He heads for the motorway and whistles as he motors along. Alive, vibrant and relishing the feeling of doing something positive, if illegal.

CHAPTER FOURTEEN - RECCE

His sitting in the lounge with the 'team' all round a table. He has updated them on the meeting with Costas, without telling them who he is, where he is or what he is. They have all decided that a visit to the airport is a necessity and today is the day. They have cups of tea in front of them, a small plate of biscuits and to all the world they look like five old friends discussing their greenfly problem or the fact that their state pension has gone up two percent under the inflation rate. Instead they are discussing the prospect of stealing a couple of million pounds.

H is holding court.

"Right, George my man, if you can hack into the flight manifest for today and see what info you can get that would be a very cool day's work.

Trisha, it's time for you to work on Margaret, drag her into lesbian heaven."

"That's disgusting. I will talk to her today. Leave it with me."

"Great. Gus, you come with me and Gilbert to Shoreham. We'll go see some planes, take some pictures and check everything out. Let's meet back here for tea."

Nods of okay and they all stand and get going.

Gus, Gilbert and H climb into H's Jag and set off for Shoreham. H is driving and Gus is riding shotgun, Gilbert lounging in the back as *Love- Alone Again Or* blasts out. Gilbert singing along. Gus looks like he's about to throw up.

"What is this shit?"

"Love." Gilbert exclaims from the back seat.

Gus spins round.

"Peace brother hippy but this is still shite."

"No you womble, the band, they're called Love, or were. Arthur Lee, one of the first racially balanced bands in history. Cool man, a really crazy band."

Gus looks at the aging hippy lying on the back seat, shakes his head and tuts.

"Jesus, what chance have we got with Frank Zappa here? We must be the Hole In The Head gang."

H chuckles beside himself. He is really starting to like these guys, more than almost anyone he's met in recent years.

They drive in silence for almost an hour. All lost in their own thoughts. As they get to the A27 H turns off the stereo. The 'boys' shuffle up in their seats and pay attention.

"Right, when we get there we'll park up and take a good look at the airport then Gus, you can take a stroll to the commercial offices and see what a plane might cost. I don't have a bloody clue. We'll just take some pictures and see if we can get a look at where the plane will land."

Gus nods.

"I'll see if I can get some brochures and prices. Must be a few planes up for sale. Price of fuel these days you've gotta be richer than Croesus just to own the bloody thing let alone fly it."

"Thank God we don't have to go too far then."

Gilbert nods in the back.

"Ain't that the truth ......Ruth."

Gus and H look at Gilbert.

"What?"

The sign on the A27 tells them they are close to the airport. H indicates and they turn into the slip road leading to Shoreham Airport.

They come to a sign:

WELCOME TO

SHOREHAM AIRPORT

THE UK'S OLDEST PUBLIC USE AIRPORT

FROM 1910 AND INTO THE FUTURE

H turns the car into Cecil Pashley Way and pulls to a halt in a lay-by. They have an uninterrupted view of the airport from the gravel covered pull-in. Half a dozen plane spotters are parked up in same place. The warm sun is making the car toasty. The sun glints off the white fuselage of a small plane taxiing along the runway.

H mops his brow with a white handkerchief, part due to the sun and part due to the close proximity of the 'end goal' he has been thinking about constantly for the entire duration of his 'retirement'.

He reaches into the glove box and removes a high spec camera with a tele-photo lens. Zooming in on the runway ahead of them he clicks the shutter repeatedly, the only sound in the car the loud click as he takes another picture.

H puts the camera into its case and turns to the team.

"Right, let's get closer then Gus and George, you go check out the planes, see if you can gauge what a Pilatus PC wotsit will cost us."

"PC 12" Gus interjects.

"Yeah, PC twelve. See if there is a second-hand dealer, if there are many available, what the delivery time will be, where we might buy one for cash. What other questions do you need to ask?"

Gus smiles at H.

"Leave that to us old pilots, I'll wing it. They will ask questions and I'll go with the flow."

H nods as if he understands.

"Ok, I'll leave it in your capables."

He turns the key in the ignition and the Jag rumbles into life.

"Me and Gil will case the rest of the place and take more pics, if we're lucky we will clock where the Pilatus will land."

He pulls the Jag back onto the road and heads toward the airport buildings. The 20 MPH signs warning him to keep to the lowest speed limit. As he approaches the first building, a helicopter sales and rental operation, he spots a parking area to his left. He looks in the mirror before indicating and is alarmed to see the mirror filled with a white car with stripes down the side, airport security. His sweat glands open and a small waterfall cascades down from his armpits. Sweat breaks out on his forehead despite the air-conditioning.

He turns into the parking area and breaths out for the first time in a couple of minutes as the security van drives on by.

"I'm too old for this shit."

Gilbert watches as the van slides past.

"He never even glanced at us."

"God. Let's get weaving."

He puts the car into park and switches off the engine.

The four old boys climb out of the car and three of them straighten their clothes. Gilbert adjusts his pony tale and flicks gravel from the toes of his sandals.

H points in the direction of the airport buildings.

"Gus, off you go, we'll take a stroll like a couple of old plane-spotters. We'll cruise around the other side after. See you back here in an hour."

"Cool. If we're late it's 'cos we're in discussion and I'll let you know. Keep your mobile on."

"Cop-you-later."

Gus and George set off in the direction of the large buildings that house helicopters and planes for sale and rent. Two old gents out for a stroll.

H leans back against the Jag and watches as they walk away. Gilbert lights up a tiny roll-up, barely two puffs worth but still too big for him to throw away.

H waits quietly as Gilbert finishes his small cigarette. Once the butt has disappeared under Gilbert's sandal H inclines his head and the two men set off round the outside of the airfield. As they walk H unslings the camera and clicks away at anything and everything.

As they walk away from the main buildings H sees a small white plane coming in to land, he points the camera at it and eventually sees it fill the lens. It is a Pilatus. H clicks a dozen shots off quickly as the small compact plane smoothly descends to the tarmac in the middle of the airfield.

H keeps clicking as the plane taxis toward a large hangar. He stops walking and stands still as he focuses on the plane coming to a rest on the tarmac. A small step ladder is quickly pushed to the side of the plane as the door opens. A man in a smart suit emerges carrying a briefcase and strides down the steps as a sleek Lexus rolls to a halt at the bottom of the steps. He reaches the bottom as a suited, cap-wearing driver opens the rear door. He steps inside the car and disappears. All this must have taken a maximum of thirty seconds. H lowers the camera, impressed.

"He must be a real hotshot. Blimey."

Gilbert agrees with him.

"I didn't think it was possible to get off a plane that quickly. It takes me twice that time to get out of bed."

"That would be true if they were unloading a 747."

"Very funny."

H smiles at Gilbert.

"Right, I've got enough shots of the plane, let's get moving."

The two men set off toward the buildings that Gus and George had headed toward. H notices that the airport is quartered into colour coded areas, Red, Yellow, Green, and Blue. They are in the Yellow area. There seems to be no security reason for the colour coding, it's no more secure in Yellow or Red than it is in Blue or Green. They continue to stroll around, casually taking pictures of everything H deems worthy.

While H and Gilbert are photographing planes Gus and George make their way to the first rental/retail outlet. They approach the doors to the charter shop and almost as if by magic the door opens and they enter. The door is being held open by a smarmy salesman. As the two old pals go through the door a hand is outstretched to shake theirs.

"Hello gentlemen. My name is Damien Stephens I am the Head of Sales here at Jupiter Aeronautics and how can I help you today."

Gus looks at him as if he has a visible disease.

"Well, we are interested in a price on a second hand Pilatus PC 12. We have a group of plane fanciers that have pooled our resources and in our dotage we want our own plane. We fly at weekends and visit places of interest and enjoy our little trips. My name is Everton Weeks."

"Like the football team?"

"No like the cricketer. And this is Mr Thomas. Jonathan Thomas. What have you got to offer?"

George turns away slightly so as not to laugh. Gus is clearly enjoying himself and is making this Salesman work.

Realising he is dealing with someone who knows their planes Damien can't smarm his way to a sale; he will have to come up with the goods. He flicks through the portfolio of stock he is holding and reads to Gus.

"Well, we have a Swiss built Pilatus, seats six to eight people plus cargo hold. It has a four blade Hartzell prop which gives you 1700 rpm.

Its 14metres 40 in length and 4 metres 26 in height. It has a wingspan of sixteen metres 23 with a cabin length of five point sixteen metres."

Gus nods sagely.

"What take-off distance over a 50 foot obstacle to do we need?"

"Oh…er…….it says 700 metres here."

Gus has him on the back foot.

"And what landing distance over a fifty foot obstacle?"

"Well…..that would be……five hundred and sixty metres."

Damien smiles, as much to himself as to Gus and George.

"What was its price new?"

"One point two million pounds."

"How long ago?"

"Twelve years."

"And what do you want for it now."

Damien slimes a smile and looks at his folder.

"Well……we have it on the books at £120,000."

Gus smiles back at him.

"Well that's a bit rich for our little group. We are not that rich."

"This is a fine plane sir. The actor Harrison Ford has one, the Royal Mounted Police use them, the US Drug Enforcement Agency has them, this is a very versatile plane."

George chips in.

"Indiana Jones, The Mounties and the Drug Busters. Means little to a group of weekend flyers like us."

Damien goes into super-slime mode.

"Well, what can you afford?"

Gus looks at him intently.

"Well, we could probably stretch to eighty."

George looks at him as if he's gone mad. Damien excuses himself and walks over to a small office on the other side of the showroom.

"Eighty thousand pounds. Are you nuts? We haven't got eighty quid usually let alone eighty thousand. I think you've fallen off the pipe you crazy old sod."

Gus looks at George and steps very close.

"We have to appear serious. H is trying to raise the cash; he says we can probably get to fifty grand. I need to keep this wazzock on the hook."

George is about to respond when the door to the office opens and Damien comes out brandishing his folder like a shield.

He walks back to Gus and George.

"I have checked the book and talked to my boss and I can go to ninety five."

Gus pulls plumber's face and sucks in air through his teeth.

"We could squeeze up to eighty five, maybe."

"We could meet at ninety."

Gus looks around.

"Can we see the plane?"

Damien smiles, he thinks he has a sale.

"It's in another hangar, can get it here tomorrow. Any good?"

"I think we can do that. What time?"

"About eleven?"

"Ok, see you back here tomorrow at eleven."

Damien shakes their hands.

They walk out the door of Jupiter Aeronautics and George wipes his hand on his trousers.

"Jesus, that guy is slimier than a bucket full of toads. Yuk."

They walk slowly back to the parking space where H's Jag is waiting with H and Gilbert resting against it in the morning sunshine.

H pushes himself off the side of the car as Gus and George approach.

"How'd it go?"

Before Gus can say anything George dives right in.

"He's fucking nuts, ninety thousand he offered that slimy creep, ninety thousand smackeroos, we haven't got a pot to piss in, in fact we haven't even got the piss in which we don't have a pot to use it."

The three other guys all look at each other. What did that mean?

George continues to rant.

"I mean, ninety thousand pounds. We are supposed to come back tomorrow and look at the bloody thing. What's the point? I mean, we can't buy it. And where did you get those names? John Thomas? You prick."

H and Gilbert laugh out loud at George's diatribe and the idea of Gus calling him John Thomas.

H opens his door.

"Come on, let's go look at a barn. I'll explain about the money in the car."

The three G's climb into the car, Gilbert and Gus still chuckling and George still muttering.

They ease out of the car park and head back to the A27. As the Jag purrs along H switches off the stereo and gets the attention of all the guys.

"Right, we have a slight problem. The job is all set up, everybody knows their place but we have a hitch. We don't have a plane. We now know where we can get one, that's a massive step forward. But, and it's a big but, we don't have the money to pay for said plane."

"No shit Sherlock." George interrupts.

H continues.

"Together we can raise about fifty grand by selling stuff, borrowing some and that leaves us forty grand light."

Silence in the car.

"I have a couple of ideas on how to raise the balance so when are you supposed to come back?"

Gus looks over at H.

"Tomorrow at eleven."

"Ok, have the meeting. What's going to happen?"

"Captain Slimebox is going to let us see the plane. We can pull it apart and get him to drop the price to about eighty thousand. He won't go below that I don't think."

"Right. Keep stringing him along. Give me a couple of weeks to get the balance."

"I'll call Drippy Damien and put him off for a few days to buy us some time. We can go back at the end of the week and string him along some more."

H indicates and pulls off the duel carriageway and heads into the Hampshire countryside. The Jag slides round the turns until they are heading down a quiet country lane. H slows the car.

"We're close, it's just up here."

H pulls into a small lay-by and switches off the engine.

They all get out of the car and cross the road to a small gate. In front of them is a large field surrounded by trees, tall poplar trees with green tops. The four men climb over the gate with a little difficulty and walk along the side of the field. Way off to the left they can see a large barn in the distance.

After almost five minutes of solid walking they are standing in front of a huge wooden barn. Two large doors in front of them have holes and cracks and the sides of the barn are covered in ivy and it has a look of having seen better days.

H looks at it and then at Gus.

"Well?"

Gus puts his hands on his hips.

"Perfect. We can definitely get the plane in there. It's easily big enough."

He turns around to look back down the field.

"Plenty of room to taxi along the field after landing. Should not cause too much grief setting down here."

H also looks back down the field.

"Is there enough room to come in over those trees at the end?"

George chips in.

"Yeah we only need five hundred and sixty metres."

Gus, H and Gilbert all turn and stare at George.

"What? I listen. I may be old but my brain still works!"

H is impressed. This is why they are doing this job. The fact that these old guys are so on the ball just reinforces H's belief that this is right.

Gus laughs.

"We have at least eight hundred metres so we have three hundred metres spare."

H turns back to the barn and walks right up to the doors. He peers inside.

"It seems to be empty. We can crack the lock and hide the plane here after the job with ease."

Gilbert lights a small cigarette.

"How did you find this place?"

H raises his eyebrows.

"It's amazing what you can find on the internet. Just tap in the right questions on Google and the world comes to you."

"Good stuff. Now all we need is the time and bottle to pull this off."

"We have both of those. It's all good."

One last look around and H inclines his head and they all set off back to the car. A good day's work completed.

———————————————————————

CHAPTER FIFTEEN – LORD TWITTY

Julian Hunter-Brown, Lord Julian Hunter-Brown as he insists on being addressed sits in his very opulent study. Leather bound, unread, books line the bookshelves. A mantelpiece with horse figurines has a portrait of 'His Lordship' hanging above it. Photos of 'His Lordship' with various celebs and royalty adorn every surface. A triumph of narcissistic glee encapsulated in one room.

He is dressed in beige corduroy trousers, a checked shirt with a yellow spotted cravat at his neck. His long hair (too long for a man of his age) flops over his collar and falls constantly over his half-rimmed glasses. He likes to think that lady bankers find him eccentric and a 'character'. Most find him affected and possibly effete.

On the floor is a wooden crate, half full with paper wrapped silverware, a jewellery box, folders, and an oak box with metal struts. This box is just about A4 size and is the most important item in the crate. The lid of the crate sits propped against a leather chair in the corner of the study. Julian Hunter-Brown has been a Lord for three years. This honour was bestowed on him for his contribution to British business. If only Her Majesty knew.

His fortune was mainly inherited from his father (also a Lord) who fraudulently acquired the land, property and wealth at the expense of others. In fact, the papers proving who really owns the large parts of Surrey and Dorset that his family claim to own, papers that prove the land and property really belong to the families of the estate workers dating back to the late 1800's are to be placed in the crate in front of the current Lord of the manor.

The reason for the urgency in getting this crate full, secure and out of sight is that an investigative journalist from The Independent has been in touch with him regarding his family history and has dubbed him "Lord Twitty" in the paper after he refused to comment on where his family fortune had been amassed and declared to her "One doesn't enquire about such things, one just goes about one's business and that's that my girl."

The journalist, Charlotte Green, was treated like a skivvy by His Lordship, he called her 'girlie, 'dear girl' and, she could hardly believe it, he even referred to her as 'totty' once. She couldn't understand why he was so defensive, patronising and rude. She referred to him as Lord Twitty in a childish but amusing dig to rattle his cage a little. It worked. He threatened all manner of retribution on the paper but her editor backed her and nothing happened. So she kept digging. She knew she was onto something.

Lord Hunter-Brown places the contents of a small, well hidden safe into the oak box. He shuts it, locks it and covers it with a purple velvet wrap. Picking up the lid of the crate from the corner he smiles like a lizard.

"Now try and find your proof girlie."

The phone on his oversized desk rings, a clanging, jarring sound from the marble based phone sitting in the ornate cradle. Leaning the crate lid against the chair he walks over the plush rug and picks up the phone.

"Lord Hunter-Brown speaking."

"Roland here your Lordship. About the pick-up for the crate. We can't do it until the nineteenth I'm afraid."

"But that's almost three weeks away."

"Well, two weeks and two days Sir."

"Stop splitting hairs my man. I need this crate picked up and taken to the airport at Shoreham as soon as possible. It is vitally important."

"The crate is booked on a flight on the….er…..21ˢᵗ. Is that right?"

"Yes, that is correct. The 21ˢᵗ at eleven thirty am."

"Well we can't deliver the crate to the holding bay until the nineteenth."

"That's ridiculous. I need it taking as soon as possible. I have no where to store this bloody thing."

"That's their rules I'm afraid, not mine."

"Well, it's preposterous. Can you store it for a few days? I am going away. I will pay you an extra hundred to pick it up tomorrow and house it until you deliver it to the airport."

A sigh from the other end of the phone.

"Ok Sir, I'll bring the van over tomorrow about ten and pick the crate up. Have the cash ready as well please."

"Very well, but don't be late."

Lord Hunter – Brown puts down the receiver.

"Prole."

He walks back to the crate and picks up the lid again. Placing the side of the lid on the corner of the crate he runs his hand over the velvet wrap. Then lowers the lid in place and selects a nail and hammer from the chair and begins to seal the lid down on his secrets.

Once the lid is sealed and he has put away his tools Lord Hunter-Brown (a.k.a. Lord Twitty) lays the paperwork for the transfer of the crate to Swiss bank *Hetlinger and Cie* on 21st May. He is pleased that the crate will be out of his house the following day once Roland picks it up.

There is a knock on the door and Lord Twitty shouts "Come"

The door opens and Lady Hunter – Brown, Cynthia, once referred to as Cynth the Nymph in upper class circles, enters her husbands study.

"What time are we leaving tonight?"

"What?"

"Tonight? Peregrine Stephens wine and book thingy. What time is it?"

"How should I know?"

"He's your bloody friend. I can't stand the man he's a pig. All his little innuendos and hands all over my bum whenever he comes near me. He's disgusting."

"He's alright. He just refers to your active past. And it's not like you've never had a hand on your bum before now is it."

"Oh yes dear, drag up anything from a past life. That stuff all happened while I was at University as you well know. Sleeping with a few boys was par for the course, as you well know because you slept with your share of boys at University as well."

"Bitch."

"Bandit."

"Sod off."

"With pleasure."

And with the final barbed comment she turns and leaves the study and her husband to stew in his own juices.

Lord Twitty walks to the window and glances out at the immaculately manicured lawn. Flourishing flower beds and the beauty of a truly magnificent English garden just one part of the sixty acres surrounding his palatial home that could all disappear if the papers contained in the crate were ever to fall into the wrong hands. Destroying them is also not an option as they are the original deeds to the property along with the bank documents that while stating that the house belongs to his family could also be used to disprove that fact.

"You're not getting me that easily totty."

CHAPTER SIXTEEN - TRAINING

The morning sun is streaming in through the large windows in the lounge and warms the room and bathes the tables in a bright glow. Nurse Phipps walks into the lounge, the hum of breakfasting residents not evident this morning. No rattle of knives, forks and spoons on plates and bowls. No idle chatter and scrape of chairs. No TV droning on in the background. She stares around the room in amazement, instead of the usual twenty or so bodies she usually herds around the lounge she is confronted by two sleeping octogenarians in the corner and seventy-six year old Fred James hanging onto his Zimmer frame as he collects his weetabix and strawberries.

She walks quickly across the lounge until she is standing beside Fred.

"Where is everyone?"

"By the pond."

"Doing what?"

"Working out apparently. They all trooped off in tracksuits and trainers about half an hour ago."

"Fuck me." She exclaims.

Fred puffs out his chest.

"Well, I'll need some jump leads and some Viagra but I'll give it a go."

Nurse Phipps looks horrified.

"Urgh, sod off you dirty old bugger."

"You started it."

She shakes her head and opens the French doors leading to the lawn and sets off in the direction of the pond.

As she marches down the lawn she follows the path down toward the pond past willow trees and large purple rhododendron bushes. As she comes round the large conifers she is confronted by a group of O.A.P.'s all doing the same exercises. They are spread out on blue mats all dressed in track suits stretching and bending. The group contains Gus, George, Gilbert and H alongside Trisha, Margaret, Ernie, Percy and Ken (still both hurling the occasional breathless insult as they roll around on the floor) and six other inmates in various stages of distress. Gus is in front yelling orders.

"One, two, one, two. Breathe. Left leg, right leg. Turn."

George is red faced and sweating, looking as though he could explode at any moment.

Gilbert is smiling like he's just smoked a joint and this is what his brain has decided he should do to relax.

Trisha looks trim and fit with her hair pulled back in a pony tail.

Margaret seems more relaxed than usual but conscious of being seen lying on the floor.

H seems comfortable working out and obviously fairly fit for a man in his sixties. He and Trisha exchange smiles every now and again. Something not lost on Margaret as they follow Gus' barked instructions.

Gus is clearly enjoying an active role in their fitness regime.

As Nurse Phipps comes round the corner and stands, hands on hips watching them H sees her and rolls onto his front and hoists himself to his feet.

"Hello Olivia. Want to join in?"

"Have you all gone loopy?"

"No, we're all just trying to stay fit for life."

"But.......but........Gilbert!"

Gilbert, lying on his back, his hands behind his head, grins up at her.

"Just chilling Miss Thrillin'."

"You never do any exercise."

"Now I aim to keep myself fit and healthy."

Gus chips in.

"Just in case, we get wealthy."

H shoots Gus a stern glance and Gus looks down.

This exchange is not lost on Olivia; she is getting a suspicious feeling creeping into her brain.

"Well, as the Nurse here I don't want you lot all coming to me with pulled muscles and sprains. You take it easy."

Gus raises his head.

"Theys all warmed up, nice routine to relax the muscles before we started Miss Phipps and we're just doing light exercise to try and help everyone a little bit."

"Ok, then be careful. I don't want to have to troop down here and deal with a heart attack."

She turns and walks away. One last glance over her shoulder as she turns past the tree line.

George calls after her, just out of earshot.

"You're all heart Miss Ratshit."

A collective laugh from the assembled exercisers.

Gus calls them all to order.

"Right, let's crack on. Trisha lass, keep that left leg straight this time."

"Time was I could put my left leg behind my left ear."

H looks over with arched eyebrows.

"Now that would've been worth seeing."

Margaret scowls at H.

"Don't be disgusting."

"Just joking Madge, chill out."

"It's Margaret, and mind your manners."

Trisha looks over at H and pulls a face that says 'stop antagonising Margaret as I have yet to persuade her to join the team' all in one glance.

The warm sun is just climbing into the sky when Gus calls a halt to the mornings exercise.

"We have all done well, same time tomorrow everyone."

The exercise crew all roll up their mats, hang towels round their necks and troop off together toward SummerVale. H walks back with Gus, just out of earshot of the rest.

"I'm going to pick up your pilot's licence later today. I've also got Trisha's passport and Margaret's passport too. We'll link up about four this afternoon when I get back."

"Fine. I'm feeling a real buzz now. Can't wait for things to move on. Is Margaret on board then?"

"Not exactly, but she will be. Trisha will swing it, you watch. It's all coming together. I feel excited and scared all at once. We are really putting it all together."

"**You** are really putting it together man."

"No, this is a team effort. We are all in this together."

"No man, since you arrived it's been amazing. The change in these people is nothing short of a miracle. Dead from the neck up, look at them now. That's all down to you. H, you are one cool dude."

"And you have been spending too much time with The Happy Hippy."

As they walk into SummerVale for their breakfast they all feel Nurse Phipps' eyes boring into them. No-one looks at her; they all just go about their business with the minimum of fuss. Nurse Phipps walks among them dispensing pills like sweets to children.

Small plastic cups with anything from one pill to a dozen for the more infirm inmates.

H is sitting with Gus and Gilbert as she approaches. She slams a cup in front of Gilbert.

As she walks away he says out loud.

"I don't even need this Viagra."

Nurse Phipps spins and returns to the table.

"Maybe not, but you'll be stiffer than ever if I find you are up to something. You're all acting very peculiar."

H smiles up at her, disarming.

"Olivia, we're only trying to make life here a bit more bearable. A bit of exercise, a bit of fun. Isn't it nice to see a few more smiling faces?"

Olivia pulls a face, thinking.

"Well, it has been a bit more cheerful here lately. But I thought it was just that Mrs Hailsham has been off sick."

Now it's her turn to smile. She has made a joke and is waiting for a response. H laughs and raises his eyebrows to encourage the others to join in. They do so.

"Naughty. You know we all love her dearly."

"Yeah right."

Nurse Phipps leaves them to their breakfast and goes on with her Florence Nightingale routine dishing out pills to one and all.

"Why do you flirt with her H? She's a nightmare."

"Gus, it's important that she doesn't get nosy. Being nice throws her off the scent. If there is a scent. We need to be as low profile as possible. She gets too inquisitive we might have a problem. I'm nice to her and she isn't used to it, you lot are mean to her and she reacts. The best way to undermine her is to be as nice as pie."

"Well she's a sneaky one. I'm sure she's been looking through my stuff."

"Gus, it's been a long time since a young woman searched through your drawers."

"That's all you know."

"What ho stud. Have another weetabix; you might need your strength."

Gilbert, quiet throughout this exchange suspends his cup halfway to his mouth.

"I think she could be hot. With a little work."

H and Gus both stare at him. Gus shakes his head and H smiles.

"Now I know you're losing the plot."

Gilbert takes a sip of his tea.

"Sweet as my tea and that's got three sugars in it."

"Sad, bad old man."

Their laughter carries across the room and Nurse Phipps looks over with undisguised suspicion at their table.

They turn away, schoolboy-like and carry on eating their breakfast.

After his happy breakfast H has a quick shower and dresses. He goes down to his car. He is about to climb into the Jag when a voice from behind makes him jump.

"Now where are you off to on such a lovely day?"

He spins around and Nurse Olivia Phipps is casually leaning against the side of the lean-to under which the Jag is stored.

"Bloody hell, will you buy some noisy shoes. It's like having a stalker on the loose."

"They come with the uniform."

"Yeah, I'm sure."

"Well? Where *are* you off to?"

"Just a bit of shopping. Any law against that?"

"Well you would know, Mister Lawyer."

H smiles and climbs into the safety of the Jag.

He turns the key and the old car rumbles into life. He looks over at Nurse Phipps but she's gone. He clicks the stereo into life and R.E.M. – *Shiny Happy People* fills the car.

"Yeah, we will be."

H pulls the car round the corner and off towards his rendezvous with Costas.

Trisha takes her bowl of cornflakes and a cup of tea and sits at a corner table next to Margaret. A very sarcastic tone conveys Margaret's disapproval of Trisha's morning exercise.

"Are you enjoying this ***working out*** ?"

"As it happens, yes. I feel fabulous."

"You look ridiculous and you are showing yourself up. Rolling around on the floor with those weirdos."

"How do you know what goes on? You have only been down to workout once. But you believe something strange is happening every morning. What? Do you think we're having an orgy by the pond every morning? Me and the three de G's and H?"

"Oh, its H now is it?"

"That's his name."

"Oooooh pardon me."

"Come on Margaret, he's a really nice bloke. We just get a little exercise, have a few laughs, I haven't felt this good in years."

"To what end?"

"I just enjoy having something to wake up for each morning."

"I have no response to that."

"Good. So just listen. I have something to tell you but it's going to freak you out and then you must make a decision but the most important thing is to let me finish and promise that what ever I tell you, you mustn't scream and you can't ever tell anyone. Agreed?"

"Ok, so now I'm really worried but I'm also intrigued. Carry on."

"In a minute we'll discuss why you're here, why no-one visits you and how we have a plan to put a lot of these things right."

"We?"

"Ah......no interrupting."

"Sorry."

"Ok. So, **we** are all working out for a reason. **We** have an idea, well H has the idea and we, that's the three de G's, me and H, are going to complete the plan and make lots of money."

Margaret's eyes widen until Trisha thinks they might pop. Trisha stops Margaret from speaking with a raised finger.

"Ahh.....no......so, we have this plan, it involves going to Switzerland, making a plane land early, landing another plane in its place and stealing a large amount of money."

Margaret emits a little squeal and puts her hand to her mouth.

They look around and no-one seems to be taking any notice of them. Trisha continues.

"So, my part in this job is to fly to Switzerland with a partner."

Trisha inclines her head and stresses the last word – partner – to convey to Margaret what she is thinking.

"then when on the plane my partner fakes a heart attack and we force the plane to land early. Meanwhile, the guys..."

"Guys?"

"Shut up and listen. They will land another plane in place of the one we force to land early."

"We?"

"Just listen will you."

"Ok."

"So, the bogus plane lands and loads up the cargo, all stuff rich people want to whisk out of the country and hide from the taxman. It's all money they want laundered and gear they want hidden from the public eye. They can't call the cops as what they are doing is bent as well."

"When did you turn into Bonnie Parker?"

"I am just giving you the information the way H explained it."

"Oh, I see."

"Do you? Well here's the deal. I am going to Switzerland and I want you to accompany me acting as my lesbian lover and then you fake having a heart attack and we force the plane to land."

"Oh is that all?"

"Well?"

"Well what, you're all barmy. You should be locked up."

"I *am* bloody well locked up, that's what we want to change. We all will get about a hundred grand each. Now that will change my last few years."

Trisha watches as the pound signs drop into Margaret's eyes. She takes a sip of tea. The silence around them growing. She decides to press on.

"And the beauty of this is that *we*, are not doing anything wrong. You can pull off the fake chest pains and I can do all the talking. We'll land somewhere, get you checked out. Fly back the following day and it'll be easy street for all of us for the rest of our days. We can travel and have fun, buy stuff. Come on, what do you think?"

Margaret pushes her cup of cold tea away from her. She is clearly fighting an inner battle, sensible Margaret against a new, improved, daring Margaret.

She purses her lips.

"So, I would just have to act like we're…..you know…… partners."

"Yes, like two old lesbo's off on a trip back to England."

"No kissing!"

"Yuk, I like you but not like that."

Margaret smiles.

"Ok, if you're in, so am I."

Trisha claps her hands together.

"Excellent. Well done Margaret, this will be brilliant."

"Mags."

"What?"

"Call me Mags, old Margaret is gone now."

"Oh Mags that's fantastic. You have to come and workout again in the morning, I'll get you a new tracksuit this afternoon."

"Can I get a blue one? I look so pale in white."

"Whatever. Let's get cracking."

They pick their cups up and set off on the first bold step to a new life.

The sun is dipping below the tree line as H pulls back into SummerVale; the bulge in his jacket pocket contains two new passports and a pilot's licence for Gus. His heart is still hammering as he has broken the law for the first time in his life. Discussing a robbery, planning a robbery, all possibly illegal but buying a false pilot's licence and two false passports – definitely illegal.

Costas had made the transaction really easy, he was very gentle with H and H felt really at ease, until he left the washeteria. Then the heart palpitations began, and still continued as he switched off the engine.

Getting out of the car, he touches his jacket pocket five times between the car and the door. Checking all around him as if The Sweeney might screech up and arrest him, (probably for looking suspicious) he ducks inside the main entrance to SummerVale and leans against the wall.

"Out of breath?"

H nearly jumps out of his skin. Nurse Phipps stands by the entrance to her office, casually leaning against the door jamb and with a very sly look on her face.

"Jesus......out of life if you do that again."

H leans back and holds his heart, plus putting his hand over the passports and licence.

"Should I check you out?"

Nurse Phipps takes a step forward.

H almost jumps out of the way.

"No, I'm fine. A little lie down will suffice."

He scoots off and up the stairs only just stopping himself running. Once inside number 68 he leans against the door until his heart stops hammering then reaches inside his jacket and throws the brown envelope onto his bed. He hangs up his jacket and removes his sweat soaked shirt. A quick underarm rinse and he pulls on a polo shirt. Back to his usual sartorial elegance he is now ready to meet the team and get ready for the next stage of their big adventure. He selects Gus' pilot's licence from the envelope, hides the package under his boxer shorts and sets off for Gus' room. A strange smile playing across his lips as he strolls down the carpeted corridor.

CHAPTER SEVENTEEN - MONEY

The morning workout comes to an end and the team, plus another four residents who have decided to join the exercise routine all pick up their towels and mats. H makes his way round the "inner circle" and tells them all to meet in his room after breakfast. They all nod agreement. The team is really pulling together. As they walk back toward SummerVale, H walks next to Margaret.

"You did well Margaret, you're very supple."

"Mags"

"What?"

"Call me Mags; and I've always been supple."

H is a little taken aback by the dramatic change in Mags; he is unsure how to respond to what could be construed as a flirtatious remark. He doesn't want to blow the change to what is the newest member of the team with an offhand remark.

"Right, okay, see you at ten."

"68"

"Eh?"

"Your room number."

"Oh yes, perfect. 68. Yeah."

H drops back as Mags links arms with Trisha as they walk back.

H drops into step with Gus.

"All ok?"

"Yeah man. All looking good. Everyone is doing well. Some quite fit old folk here."

"That's good news."

"Hope they are as fit mentally."

"Yes. Have you got the licence somewhere safe?"

"It's in an old sock in my bag. It'll take a very strong nose to dig around in there. A reet stink if tha' knows what I mean."

"What do we need to sort your uniform out?"

"We can pick up a uniform anywhere, it's the badge and insignia we need."

"I have a photo of the pilot from before; I have blown up the photo so we can get a copy done next week. Can you get the uniform later this week?"

"No problem…..but I'm getting a bit low on cash."

"Yes, I know. We need to talk about that after breakfast."

"Ok. I need a shower before we meet up."

H accelerates a bit and over his shoulder calls.

"Don't forget to wash your feet."

"Bollocks."

"Them too."

They head into the breakfast room with the rest of the team and all sit around two tables pushed together. Something that doesn't go unnoticed by Nurse Phipps standing by the pill trolley waiting to dispense tablets to those in need.

Just after ten thirty the assembled crew are crammed into H's room. Mags and Trisha sit on one side of the bed, Gilbert and Gus on the other. George sits on the edge of the bed his feet planted on the floor, H is pacing, and Gus is on the chair. H opens his boxer short drawer and lifts the Calvin Klein's on the right. The envelope is not there. He scrabbles under the pants and puts his hand to the left hand side of the drawer and sighs as he feels the envelope. He removes the package and shuts the drawer. He stops and thinks. He is stationary for a long time. He shakes his head.

"I know I put this envelope under my pants on the right hand side of this drawer, I'm certain of it. Someone has definitely been in here. I know that."

He looks at the others. They are all just staring at him.

"Well?"

Gus shrugs his shoulders. George purses his lips. Trisha and Mags look at each other. Gilbert tugs at his beard and reacts vocally to the statement from H while everyone else considers the implications.

"So, who would be nosing through your stuff? Hailsham? Ratshit? Anyone else been nosing about?

H thinks about this.

"Not that I can think of. No-one takes any notice of me. Ratshit has been a bit busy lately though. She always seems to be around. Every time I turn around she seems to be right behind me."

"What does this mean? What could she know?"

H waves the passports in the air.

"She could know that Trish and Mags have false passports. But what could that mean? She might think they are leaving here but that's all. Let me think about this."

H is pacing, talking to himself almost.

"She can't make any sense of this. There is nothing else in there. Let's forget it, move on."

Trisha stands up.

"Are you sure?"

"Yes, it's fine. If she asks you anything just tell her they are fakes that I picked up for a laugh."

"Will that work?"

George chips in.

"What else can she think? She's a pain in the butt and a miserable cow but she ain't that bright."

H offers his opinion.

"Don't underestimate her. I think she's bright enough. Just everyone be on their toes."

Trisha sits back down. H hands Trisha and Mags their new passports. They both open them.

"Margaret Stein. I'm not Jewish."

The others laugh.

"Patricia Sappho. What the hell sort of name is that?"

H chokes back his laughter as he tries to explain.

"Sappho was a Greek poet that came from the Island of Lesbos and wrote love songs and sonnets to women. She lived around 600BC. The first lesbian?"

"Ha bloody ha. We are only playing at being a couple you dozy twonk."

The boys are all in fits of laughter. Mags is getting a bit annoyed.

"What's Stein mean? Are you saying I look like Frankenstein?"

"No, Mags, I promise."

"Well, what does it mean?"

Trisha answers.

"Gertrude Stein was a very famous lesbian writer in Paris in the 30's and 40's a very butch lesbian."

"You bastard H."

H looks to say sorry to Mags but sees that she is smiling.

The laughter subsides and H continues.

"Right, serious stuff."

H opens a folder and hands each of them a typed A4 sheet. He waits while they all read it through.

"So, you can see, we need to raise £100,000."

Gilbert whistles.

"Well, there goes the dream."

Trisha turns on Gilbert and responds tersely.

"No, we can ***not*** give up yet."

H turns and tapes a sheet on the wardrobe with some cello tape so all can read it. He takes a black marker pen and writes on the sheet.

```
PLANE -      80,000
FUEL -       10,000
PASSPORTS -   1000
PILOTS LICENCE -   500
FLIGHTS TO SWITZ -   200
FLIGHTS TO UK -   5000
O/NIGHT SWITZ -   200
UNIFORM -    300
OTHER -     2800
_____

         100,000
```

The team all stare at the sheet. No-one speaks as H then takes a second sheet and sticks this next to the costs sheet. H writes everyone's name on the sheet, he starts with his own, then Gus, then Gilbert, then George, then Trisha and finally Mags.

H then writes £30,000 against his own name. He turns to Gus.

"What can you raise Gus?"

"Probably £5000, maybe 7 if I beg."

H scribbles £5000 against Gus' name.

"Gil?"

"Three K, if I'm lucky."

"George?"

"Five tops."

"Trish?"

"Maybe three?"

H writes the figure in.

"Mags?"

"Two, with a fair wind."

H writes it against her name. A quick tot up and he totals everything and writes £ 48,000 at the bottom.

Gus wipes his hands on his trousers.

"I can ask a few old mates and I'll talk to my boy. He might finally decide to talk to me. Put me down for eight grand."

H turns the five into an eight next to Gus' name.

Gilbert pulls a face and tells H. "Put me up to five then."

George says nothing, just shrugs his shoulders.

Trisha lifts her face to H.

"I might be able to go to about seven; I need to make a few calls."

Mags joins in too.

"I can sell a few things. Put me down for five."

H changes all the figures and tots the columns up.

"So, that takes us to sixty, we're forty k short."

H looks crestfallen.

"Where are you getting thirty grand from H?"

"It's about time I got rid of that gas guzzler outside. Time to get a car that's cheaper to run anyway."

"You can't sell that car, you love it."

"I want to do this thing a lot more than I want a large car that sits under a lean-to day in day out."

George is a picture of defeat but presses on.

"So what are we going to do?"

H puffs out his cheeks.

"Right, everyone go and see what they can raise and let's meet tomorrow same time and see where we are."

They all stand and walk to the door. After they have left H leans with his back to the door and closes his eyes. The pain of failure is intense and H has held it in while the others were with him but it all crashes in and makes him feel old and useless.

A few minutes pass and he girds his loins and talks to himself.

"Come on, let's go, we can do this."

H picks up his keys and slips on his shoes. He marches out of number 68 with a determined strut. Down the stairs and out the door to the Jag.

Nurse Phipps watches from the window as H pulls across the gravel driveway in his car. She turns with a smile on her face and heads for the stairs.

CHAPTER EIGHTEEN - OLIVIA

The door to number 68 opens silently and Olivia Phipps steps inside quickly and closes the door behind her. Her heart is beating very fast. Although she has every right to check the rooms as the Nurse on-site, this is a bit different. She has an agenda for being in here. She composes herself and starts to look around the room; all seems to be normal until her eyes stop on the two sheets stuck on the wardrobe doors. She walks over and takes a closer look.

"Interesting."

She runs her finger down the list and then across to the costs list.

"What on earth?..."

She turns and opens the top drawer of H's chest of drawers, rummages around, finds nothing. Second and third drawers the same. At the bottom of the fourth drawer she finds an A4 folder which she removes. It contains H's A4 pad, pages and pages of scribbled notes, timetables, numbers, weather reports, and details of plane markings. She is confused until she turns another page and the job timetable is laid out in black and white. She takes a few minutes to read the full detail and shakes her head in amazement.

She drops the folder on the bed and opens the wardrobe doors. She pushes jackets and trousers hanging up to one side and removes a rolled up map which she opens.

"Switzerland."

She ducks in again and removes the white cardboard sheet with lots of photos attached. She lays it on the bed and runs her eyes over each picture.

"Well bugger me."

"I'd rather not."

She jumps away from the bed and holds her hand to her heart. She has not heard H returning and opening the door. He is standing just inside the door looking right at her.

"That's private."

"You are planning a robbery."

"It's a film script I'm working on, we all are."

"I don't believe you."

"So what, it's the truth."

"Truth my arse, you have too much detail here, too much knowledge."

She points to the list of names and money next to each name (the reason H returned as he remembered he hadn't tidied up) and then back at H.

"All contributing to a good cause? All putting money into a pot to write a script? All planning a way out of here more like."

"So what? We've done nothing wrong. We can all dream, even this place can't take our dreams away."

Olivia stares long and hard at H. He stares right back.

"So, what now? You going to tell the authorities – (he adopts a falsetto voice like a high pitched queeny squeal) 'oh officer, several of the old farts in my concentration camp have been planning a robbery, I have all the detail, come and take them away, is there a reward?' – or are you just going to tell us to behave? Or maybe blackmail us into giving you some of the money *if* we pull it off?"

"Can you?"

"What?"

"Pull it off?"

H is sent a little sideways by the conversation, he wasn't expecting a discussion.

"I think so, we need a bit more info and some more work…."

"And some more money?"

Olivia points to the finance sheet totalling sixty thousand pounds. The other sheet showing one hundred thousand pounds needed.

"Forty grand by the look of it."

"You have been nosy."

"Well you left it all on show didn't you?"

"But not the stuff in my drawers and wardrobe. And by the way, when you nose around in my underwear kindly put things back in the correct place."

"Sorry."

"What do you mean bloody sorry. Nosing around in private stuff is not part of your job description I don't think."

"I mean, sorry if I disturbed your things. Curiosity got the better of me, seeing you all together."

"No, a cat is curious, and you know what happened then. Plato once said 'To be curious about that which is not one's concern while still in ignorance of oneself is ridiculous'!"

"Well as you said, curiosity killed the cat but I was a suspect for a while…..Steven Wright said that and he never wore a toga."

Olivia smiles to try and diffuse the situation but H is still stony faced.

"So, what happens now?"

"Sit down."

H stays exactly where he is.

"Please."

He relents and goes and sits in his chair.

Olivia starts to pace a little, her white nurses' shoes squeaking slightly with every step.

"So, we have a situation."

"No shit Shirley."

"You and the dream team are planning to rob an aeroplane but haven't got enough money to finance your needs. Right?"

"Well, yes. If we had any money we wouldn't be here in shithole central now would we?"

"So, tell me all the details and I'll decide what to do."

"Why? If I tell you any more than you have already sneakily found out then it just compounds our situation."

"Please trust me. Just tell me everything."

"Trust you! You've been rummaging in my drawers and want me to trust you."

Olivia can't help herself. She starts to giggle.

"It's not bloody funny."

Then H can't contain himself either, he starts to laugh.

They wait until their joint chuckle-fest subsides and with H sitting in the chair, Olivia moves the papers away and sits on the edge of the bed.

H then tells her the full story, start to finish. From the court hearing to the cells, to the lock – up (he doesn't tell her about Costas), training, planning, the recce, the plane, the cost, what might be in the crates, the full details of everyone's involvement. Somehow, he senses she might not be as judgemental as he would have expected.

H finishes with a sigh.

"So that's the full story, warts and all."

"And these rich wankers have been spiriting their loot out of the country like this for years?"

"Apparently so."

"Bastards."

"Well, no-one likes paying tax."

"That's true."

Olivia takes a moment and then looks right into H's eyes.

"Right. You've told me a really interesting and potentially damaging story. I asked you to trust me and you did. Now it's my turn."

"Ok."

H is unsure where this is all going.

"I am thirty eight years old. Never been married. Got engaged once, turned out he was gay. My life is tied up in this place, almost as much as you lot. I have no life outside, no friends really. I have no family except a barking mad Aunt who lives in a small cottage near West Cork in Ireland and I hate my life."

H just nods.

"I have never broken the law, not since College anyway, and I think I'm a decent person. I'm nothing like Nurse Ratched in Cuckoo's Nest, although Louise Fletcher won an Oscar for that role, wouldn't mind that. Anyway, I digress; I have a proposition for you. I'll put up the balance of the money but I want in."

She waits for an argument but H just sits there with his mouth open so she pushes on.

"A lovely old lady called Grace, a long term resident whose family abandoned her, left me a decent chunk of change a couple of years ago. I have been trying to decide what to do with it. I felt it was inappropriate to just buy stuff so I wanted to use it. Grace had such spark; she would have loved this idea when she was fully functioning."

H blinks his eyes a few times, shakes his head in disbelief.

"Well."

"Well what?"

"Well yes, welcome on board."

"Great, so, I have an idea."

H's face changes completely. This is the producer joining a film and re-writing the entire script.

Olivia sees the look on his face and cuts him off at the pass.

"Just a small idea. Hear me out."

"Ok."

H crosses his arms in a very defensive posture.

Olivia continues.

"The most expensive part of this plan and it's a great plan by the way."

Defensive posture relaxes a bit.

"Is the cost of the plane. Right?"

H nods at the list on the wardrobe.

"Yep."

"So why buy a plane."

"Well, we need one for the plan to work."

"Okay, I realise that. But why not **rent** one for two weeks at half the cost, or whatever that might be, paint it, give it back, no-one will know any different. And we can save ourselves a shed load of cash."

H takes on board her use of we, it makes him relax a whole lot more. He digests what she has said.

"You, young lady, are a bloody marvel. That's genius."

H reaches forward and takes her face in his hands and kisses her gently on the lips. An affectionate kiss not a sexual kiss. At that moment the door opens and Gus walks in.

"Jesus bloody Christ. H, what the hell are you doing?"

H drops Olivia's face and stands up quickly.

"Gus, it's not what it seems."

Olivia joins in.

"No it's bloody well not."

"Well it looked like summat to me."

"Gus, come in, we've got a lot to tell you."

"We?"

"Yes, we. Trust me, sit down."

Gus suspiciously walks into the room after closing the door. He sits on the edge of the bed away from Olivia. He looks at the bed and sees all the papers spread about, the map and the photos. He rubs his hand over his head a few times as if trying to shake a thought free.

"So, I set off to go and see about flogging the Jag. Completely lost my marbles and left everything out on view. Remembered that I hadn't put everything away when I was about ten miles away. Turned around and came back to find Miss Nosy Breeches here up to her eyes in all the information."

"Thought as much."

"No you didn't, you thought we were misbehaving, didn't you."

"You still might be."

"Shhh. So, I caught her red handed. She asked me to explain the whole story, so I did."

"You did what? Why? What about us?"

"Just listen. I had no choice."

"I gave him no choice Gus."

"Charming."

H motions for them both to be quiet.

"So, after telling her the full story, Olivia…"

Gus' eyebrows raise so high they almost leave his head.

"Olivia explained her circumstances. She is as much an inmate as us. She has also agreed to put in the balance of the money we need, but, and this is a big but, she has come up with a genius idea to make this all do-able. Tell him Olivia."

Gus turns his head to Olivia and waits for the oracle to reveal itself.

"Well, I saw the financial breakdown and it was quite obvious that buying the plane is the biggest outlay for us."

"Us?"

She ignores Gus and carries on.

"The fact that we need the plane to complete the mission is obvious, but we don't need to own it. We can **rent** one."

She lets that statement hang in the air and watches Gus' face as her idea permeates his brain.

Gus smiles.

"That's brilliant."

"That's why I kissed her."

"Don't I get a kiss from you then Gus?"

Gus leans forward and puckers up. Closes his eyes and waits. Olivia leans forward and pecks him on the lips. H laughs.

"Oi, get a room. How much do you think it will cost to hire or rent a plane for two weeks?"

Gus replies.

"A lot less than eighty grand I can assure you. Probably ten grand a week."

Olivia stands.

"Then we're all set. I have twenty five waiting to be used. I'll get it tomorrow and we can get cracking."

"Ok, if you and Gus can get to Shoreham and see the sales guy in a week or so that will be a major step taken in the right direction. I'll sort two new passports and you will be able to do the deal with a bit of secrecy. Gus, do you want to talk to your man with the plane? I will get the others on-side and we'll have a meeting tomorrow to nail down who does what over the next few days. We have…."

H picks up his diary and checks the dates.

"……sixteen days until D-Day on the 21st. We have to make sure everything is ready well in advance."

"Ok, I will need my uniform checked and then the insignia stitched on. I think it would be good for Olivia to come on board as the stewardess. What do you think?"

"What me as a trolley dolly? I don't think so."

"Come on, it will be fun."

H knows they have her hooked.

"Come on Olivia, it might make sense to have an extra body on board."

"Oh ok, this has taken on a whole new dimension now."

"But it's gonna be such fun."

"We'll see. I might throw up."

Gus laughs.

"It's the stewardesses' job to clean that stuff up."

"Yuk. No puking then, from anyone."

H starts to put all the charts, maps and files away. Gus and Olivia realise the meeting is over.

H turns to them both.

"Let's all meet here at eleven tomorrow. Will that give you enough time to do your rounds Olivia?"

"Plenty. I'll need to get weaving this afternoon but the bank in town is only ten minutes away. Eleven tomorrow is fine."

"See you then. Let's keep everything under wraps for now."

Olivia walks round the bed and when she gets level with H she leans up and kisses him on the cheek.

"Thanks."

H smiles at the gentle affection.

Gus and Olivia leave. H touches his hand to his cheek.

He keeps smiling to himself as he puts away all traces of the job the team are planning.

CHAPTER NINETEEN – PREPARATION

Eleven o'clock on the dot next day and the team assemble in H's room. H has let everyone in when a tap on the door makes everyone turn and look. Olivia is the only one not there yet. H opens the door and Olivia is standing outside in the corridor. H ushers her in. Smiles and hellos all round. H shuts and locks the door.

"Right, here we go. I have got twenty six grand in this parcel. A quick sale of the old Jag this morning, replaced with a Swedish box but what the hey"

He throws a jiffy bag on the bed.

Olivia throws her package on top of it.

"There's another thirty there. Twenty five from old Grace and five from my savings."

Trisha pitches in with five, Mags with four and Gus with three. George throws four on the bed and Gilbert puts his sandaled foot on the edge of the bed and removes a wedge from his sock, throws it on the pile, he does the same with the other leg, then reaches into his trousers and throws another brick of used noted on the bed.

Everyone watches and let out a collective. "Eeeuuwwww."

Gilbert just looks at them.

"It's all money."

H asks.

"How much?"

"Three and a half."

H does a quick calculation.

"Seventy four and a half."

Trisha corrects him.

"Seventy five thousand five hundred actually."

"Ok, so, what do we need to spend straight away? Trish, take seven K and get the flights for you and Mags. Can you pay cash at the travel agent?"

"No problem, spoke to them already. They have secured us two seats we need to go and pay for them tomorrow, we will need to go to Alton to buy two tickets to Switzerland then book a hotel for the night before."

"Great stuff Trish, you and Mags can finish off your job tomorrow."

Trisha nods at H and smiles.

"Gil, how much are you going to need to buy the van, cash, no questions asked?"

"I'll need a grand and I'm going to get a van and an old banger then switch registration numbers. I have identified the van, need to do that soon, in case any work needs to be done on the van, we don't want it breaking down on the way back from the barn."

"Oh no, we don't want that."

H looks around the room.

"Let's go! Gil you go sort the van. Trisha and Mags I'll drive you to town so you can get your tickets. Olivia, you and Gus can get your uniforms tomorrow morning and then I'll drive you to Shoreham for the plane. That will give us a clear ten days before we're due to actually do this."

Everyone falls silent as they realise it's really going to happen.

They set off on their various quests. Olivia takes the bag now containing sixty six thousand pounds and locks it in her pharmacy cupboard. H walks down to his 'new' Volvo with Mags and Trisha and they head for town and a date with the travel agent.

Their new life is starting to loom large on the horizon.

The following morning Gus and Olivia are in H's Volvo heading for the fancy dress shop in the local town to pick up their uniforms. H is buzzing.

"Gilbert has stashed the van, a bloody white van if yer don't mind, behind the greenhouse. Trisha and Mags have their tickets for Switzerland and also the tickets for the Pilatus back from Lugano. We now have to get you two uniformed up, rent a plane and somewhere to stash it and we're good to go."

Gus turns away from the window and looks at H.

"Trisha and Mags are going to sew the insignias on tonight. We'll be all set then."

They pull up outside Jenny's Costumes and Gus and Olivia get out. H parks round the corner and walks back down the High Street.

Inside the fancy dress shop Gus and Olivia look through the hundreds of uniforms, from Cinderella to Charlie Chaplin, from Adolf Hitler to Attila the Hun, this place has them all.

Gus finds the perfect blue serge uniform, he picks it off the rail and walks to the counter.

"Can I try this on please?"

The teenage girl behind the counter is so engrossed in her conversation on her mobile phone that she just waves in the general direction of the back of the shop. Gus walks back with his uniform and finds a small cubicle with a sheet covering the entrance. He walks in and sets about trying it on.

Olivia picks up a pure white 'South Pacific' style uniform and holds it up to her chest. She looks in the mirror and sees a strip-o-gram and replaces the uniform. A little further along the rail she selects a blue uniform and once again holds it up against her body. It fits the bill. She walks to the back of the store and finds a second changing room. Gus is looking at himself in the mirror when the curtain is pulled back and Olivia steps out looking like a real stewardess. Gus whistles.

"My Lord. You look like a real stewardess. Gorgeous."

"And you look like a handsome flyer Gus."

"Well thank you kindly ma'am."

Gus removes his jacket and looks at Olivia.

"Right, let's get these hired and get going."

"Ok."

They exit the shop carrying their uniforms in plastic carry cases and spot H reading a paper standing on the corner of the street. As Gus approaches he can't help having a dig at H.

"Who do you think you are Sam Spade?"

"I feel more like Bumphrey Hogart. How'd it go?"

"Great, got both uniforms rented for two weeks under my new name so we don't have to return them. Cash deposit left. Let's get them back to home."

"What's yours like Olivia?"

"Lovely, I feel like a proper stewardess in it."

They walk back and climb into the old Volvo and set off for SummerVale.

Inside the car, H is thinking and speaks his thoughts aloud.

"So, just the plane to sort tomorrow and we're ready."

"Bloody hell."

Both men turn and look at Olivia in the back.

"Bloody hell is right."

Back at SummerVale Trisha and Mags are put to work stitching the insignia that Gus has procured from the airport trade counter. They sit in the lounge by the window Trisha sewing Gus' and Mags looking after Olivia's. The rest of the team are sitting round, occasionally getting tea, taking it in turns to enquire if anyone wants anything. A really genial, relaxed, friendly atmosphere.

When the stitching is complete the jackets are handed over and the group all depart for their own rooms. H and George watch as Gus and Olivia depart, H calls out to them both.

"See you after breakfast. We'll get going about ten. Ok?"

Gus and Olivia nod assent and head out of the lounge. H turns to his companion.

"Right George, time to go. You ready to crack their site?"

"Well, I need to talk to you about that."

H feels his blood turn cold and his insides freeze.

"What do you mean? Don't tell me you can't do it? If that's the case we are royally cattle-trucked."

George lifts his head and his face turns from solemn to smiling.

"Of course not you twit, I have already been in twice. They really don't have a decent firewall and I can crack it in minutes. I will be ready to get the landing codes and details on the morning of the job. Don't worry it's a piece of piss."

H rubs his head.

"Don't worry, don't bloody worry, I am nearly ready for my heart attack. Even if we pull this off I will end up in the Intensive Care Unit at the local hospital. You bugger. Glad that's all sorted though. Nearly ready now. Just a bit of prep and we can start to dream."

"It'll happen, its genius. Trust me I'm a doctor."

H smiles at his friend.

"I'm knackered. Off to bed."

"I'm going to have a nightcap then hit the stairs."

H stands and leaves George to find a drinking buddy and heads upstairs.

CHAPTER TWENTY - SHOREHAM

Gus and Olivia are sitting in the breakfast room finishing their morning cuppa when H approaches the table.

"You ready? I'll drive you to the airport."

He looks at Olivia.

"You got the cash?"

"Safe in my bag. I'm nervous carrying this much money though."

"It'll be fine. You've got Joe Frazier's big brother looking after you."

"Who?"

"Forget it. Generational conflict."

Gus and Olivia stand and follow H out to his car. The classic Jag is gone and in its place standing under the lean to at the side of SummerVale is a twenty year old Volvo.

"Ah man, it seems wrong that the Jag is gone."

"I'll buy another one when we're done. Don't worry."

They all climb in and set off for Shoreham.

Chugging along the A27, H is humming along to The Clash – *I Fought The Law* and Gus is nodding his head. Olivia is sitting in the back tapping her toes.

"Maybe a piece of crap but the stereo is good."

The sign for the airport comes up and H turns gently into the slip road and parks up alongside a few other plane spotters and switches off the engine.

H turns in his seat and looks at both Gus and Olivia.

"I think you should walk from here and go see the sales guy."

"Ok. Wish us luck."

Gus and Olivia leave the old Volvo and set off in the bright sunshine towards the airport buildings.

H leans back and closes his eyes.

A tap at the window rouses H from his nap. He looks up to see what looks like a twelve year old policeman smiling in at him. He rubs his face and winds down the window.

"Hello sir, is everything ok?"

"Yes thank you officer. Just closing my eyes for five minutes."

"Ok sir, nothing illegal about that. Just checking."

"Just tired. You get that way when you get old. You'll find out one day."

"I understand sir."

"I very much doubt that but then what's new."

The young copper realises H is being a bit short with him. He's not best pleased.

"There's no need to be like that sir, I was just making sure you were alright."

"Why, because I might have died in my sleep here at the wheel?"

"No sir, just a precaution, your age has nothing to do with it. It's a good place to sleep off a drink or two."

"It's not even lunchtime yet!"

"That sir has nothing to do with anything. I am just doing my job."

"Harassing O.A.P's is not in your job description as far as I know. I'm sure the Police Complaints Commission would be very interested in asking why you insisted rousting a kindly old gentleman who was doing nothing wrong while a convertible BMW X3 flies along the airport perimeter road at least twice the legal speed."

"Where?"

"Behind you *officer* . Now let me go back to my nap."

H winds up his window and closes his eyes. The young policeman doesn't quite know what to do so he wanders off in search of a crime to solve leaving H to snooze in the sunshine.

Meanwhile Gus and Olivia walk into the showroom of Jupiter Aeronautics, as they do so Olivia threads her arm through Gus'. He almost jumps out of his skin.

She whispers in his ear.

"Relax, I'm just arm candy. You're in charge, remember, he needs the sale more than we need the plane."

"Yeah right."

They cross the showroom and pass under the wing of a small two-seater plane.

Gus looks at the gleaming, brand new single wing machine and runs his eyes over its sleek lines.

"Decathlon, two-seater, beautiful."

"You can buy one soon."

"I wish."

They walk across to the small office. As they approach the slimy salesman appears sensing a sales opportunity and walks forward with his hand outstretched. Gus extricates himself from Olivia and shakes the limp hand and forces a smile.

"Hello again. Mr Weeks isn't it?"

Gus wipes his hand on the back of his trousers as he replies.

"Yes, that's right. We are here to close a rental deal on that Pilatus. Need it for two weeks and somewhere to house it as we discussed on the phone."

Damien Stephens smells money and moves into sales mode.

"As I explained we have just the plane you require, did you get my email? "

"Yes, it looks perfect. We just need to discuss a price for the rental."

"Do you have your licence?"

Gus reaches into his pocket and removes the licence Costas has sorted out for H. He hands it over for Damien to look at.

"That's great. Thanks. Come into the office. Can I get you a drink?"

"No thank you".

Olivia adopts a really 'girlie' voice.

"I'd love a glass of wine."

Gus glares at her, she just smiles back.

They enter the messy office and Damien moves a pile of files from a chair and offers the seat to Olivia, she sits.

"Right, let me get the lady a glass of wine and we'll check out the rental book."

He goes into a small kitchen off to the side and Gus and Olivia hear a glass being filled. He emerges carrying a glass of white wine which he hands to Olivia.

He walks round his desk and pushes piles of papers out of the way and picks up a large brown file. He opens it and flicks through the dog-eared pages until he finds the ones he wants.

"Pilatus, yes….PC 12…yes, here we are. Two weeks you say?"

"That's right."

"Book price is fifteen thousand a week plus fuel."

Gus whistles. Gives the plumbers shake of the head.

"Bit too dear really."

"How much have you got in your budget?"

Gus flicks a glance at Olivia who acts as if her wine is something a lot nicer than the supermarket plonk it actually is.

"About eight a week was what we had planned to spend."

Damien shakes his head.

"Way too cheap I'm afraid."

Gus takes the glass from Olivia's dainty hand and pulls her gently to her feet.

"Fair enough, we'll try elsewhere."

Damien flies into sales saving mode.

"Whoa, hold up; let's see what we can do. How about ten a week plus your fuel."

Gus is enjoying the cut and thrust of the sale environment.

"How about twelve grand a week and the fuel is your cost?"

"Hmmm."

"And we'll need to rent a hangar for the two weeks as well."

Damien rummages around in another file and then closes it with a flourish.

"Here's my best offer. Twelve thousand a week for the plane including fuel and a thousand a week for the hangar, paid in advance."

Gus smiles.

"You've got a deal."

"How would you like to pay?"

Olivia, standing just behind Gus chips in.

"Will cash be okay?"

Damien lets a snake-like smile play across his lips.

"That'll do nicely."

Gus wants this over.

"Draw up the paperwork and we'll take a look at the hangar. When will the plane be delivered?"

"It's on the far side of the airport. We'll refuel it and move it across either tomorrow or Thursday. That ok?"

"Fine."

Olivia opens her bag and counts out twenty thousand pounds then a smaller pile of six thousand pounds.

"Can we get a receipt please?"

"Of course my dear."

A short while later the three of them walk across the tarmac to a large hangar just to the left of the main buildings. A perfect spot for their needs.

"You access the hangar by a code; it gets changed every time the hangar gets let out. Your code is 67419, I've written it down here for you."

He hands Gus a small piece of paper with the code scribbled down.

The vast hangar stands empty and they just peek inside.

Olivia pulls Gus away.

"Come on hun, we've got to get going. You can come and play planes next week."

Gus raises his eyebrows at Damien.

"Women eh. Can't live with them, can't staple their lips together."

Damien half chuckles.

"You go on, I'll lock up here."

Gus shakes his hand once more.

"Thanks a lot. Be back at the weekend."

"Fabulous. Thanks a lot."

Gus and Olivia link arms once again and stroll off in the warm sunshine and head back to the car parking area.

Gus and Olivia get back in the car. Olivia sinks back into the rear seat. Gus has a big grin on his face. H looks at Gus.

"Well? How did it go?"

"Fine. A bit sticky but Olivia played the rich bitch to the hilt. Cool as....we're taking delivery day after tomorrow and it will be housed in hangar forty two ready for us to prepare for our jaunt."

"How much?"

"Twenty four grand rent plus a grand a week for the hangar. Twenty six grand in all, all paid up."

Olivia chips in from the back waving a piece of paper.

"We have a receipt too."

"Excellent stuff. Let's get out of here. Had a nosy bizzy round here trying to breathalyse me. Coppers, bunch of arseholes."

H switches on the engine and they pull away from the parking area.

"What is the collective noun for a group of arseholes? You have a murder of crows, a pride of lions, a school of whales, what would it be for arseholes?"

H catches Olivia's face in the rear view mirror, a huge grin on her face.

"A clench?"

"A clench of arseholes. Hmmm."

"A ringpiece?"

Gus laughs out loud.

"A buttock of arseholes."

"A posterior of arseholes?"

They are all howling with laughter.

"You guys crack me up."

Olivia talks through her laughter.

"That's it – a crack of arseholes."

H shakes his head.

"Let's get back before we all get arrested."

H pulls back onto the duel carriageway and they head back towards their HQ.

CHAPTER TWENTY ONE - PLANE

Gus walks into H's room and knocks on the open door as he comes in.

"Hello, got a minute?"

"Of course."

Gus sits down.

"Right, I've booked a spot at a small airfield in Surrey, it's about ten minutes flying time and half an hour in the car getting there. We've got the spot for a week. Hangar included for seven hundred pounds. I will fly the plane there tomorrow and we can start work preparing to change the registration."

"Great work Gus. We're almost ready."

"It feels so real now. I get butterflies every time I think about what we're going to do."

"Yeah, me too. So explain how you think we can get away with the registration change?

"Well, we will paint the number on a large white sheet stuck over the real registration and then after the job we just rip off the fake i.d. and we are back to the original registration. Simple."

"Oh yeah, simple. Will it work?"

"We need two large sheets of very sticky white paper to paste over the registration and we're in business."

H reaches into his small holdall under the bed and removes a wad of money. He counts out two thousand pounds and hands it to Gus.

"Take this; just bring me back the change."

Gus stands.

"I'll go book a time slot to take the plane out tomorrow. I'll pay the rent for the hangar in cash and we'll need picking up late in the afternoon. We can buy the sticky paper on the way back. There's a large B&Q somewhere close I'm sure. Here's the address of the airfield."

Gus hands H a piece of paper with the address on it.

" See you later."

"Bye."

Gus leaves and H continues to make notes in his little pad. He slips the address into his pocket.

Another knock on the doorframe and Gilbert fills the frame.

"Got a minute?"

"Come in, revolving door policy today. "

Gilbert sits in the seat vacated by Gus.

"I will need to buy some brushes and Gus has pointed me in the direction of a shop that sells special airplane paint. It's quite expensive though."

H reaches into his holdall once again. He takes out a collection of notes, about five hundred pounds.

"Enough?"

"Plenty. Me and Gus are going there this afternoon to buy a few tins and the brushes."

"Great stuff."

Gilbert stands and goes to leave.

"Cop-you-later."

"Bye."

Later in the evening they all sit round a table listening to *Ronnie Gale and his Magic Organ* play Abba covers, this time with his beautiful assistant Marie (a fifty year old bottle blonde from Rayleigh in Essex with a voice like a foghorn) and apart from cringing as they murder *Waterloo* they discuss where they are in terms of the job.

H holds court. He looks at each member as he outlines the state of play.

"Right, Mags and Trish have tickets to Switzerland and tickets back to Shoreham, new passports and new togs for their identities. Gus has his uniform, licence and passport. Paper for side of the plane is in the van. Plane being moved tomorrow. Gil has brushes and paint for new registration. Van is stashed behind the greenhouse. George has his computer all ship shape ready to hack into the Shoreham computer next Thursday morning. I have the Volvo parked outside ready for action. So, when the plane is in situ at new hangar we'll all go there over the weekend and prep it. Everything is ready. Just got to hope the weather is ok and that they actually are moving some stuff next Thursday."

Everyone stops and stares at him as Ronnie and Marie destroy *Dancing Queen*. No-one had considered the fact that there might not be any stuff being spirited away.

Trisha closes her eyes.

"So, we might do this and no cash and stuff will be on the plane?"

"Well, that's a possibility. A remote one, but still a possibility."

"Bugger."

"George will hack in over the weekend and check the manifesto. It should be booked in and we'll know what cargo they will be booked to pick up."

"Great, hold our breath over the weekend. Pray the rich bastards have goodies to move."

"Correct."

Trisha stands.

"I need a lie down. I'm going to bed."

She leaves and Mags follows. The boys all sit and listen as Ronnie plays and Marie screeches through *Money, Money, Money*. H shakes his head in disbelief.

"On that note I'm off to bed. See you guys tomorrow."

H walks out of the lounge with Abba's words and Marie's squeal ringing in his ears:

'A man like that is hard to find but I cant get him off my mind
Aint it sad
And if he happens to be free I bet he wouldnt fancy me
Thats too bad
So I must leave, Ill have to go
To Las Vegas or Monaco
And win a fortune in a game, my life will never be the same...'

"Oh shit."

The breakfast room is slowly filling up as H walks in. Gus and Olivia are both visible. Gus sitting by the window, Olivia handing out pharmaceuticals. Gilbert and George are loitering by the tea urn. H walks over and George spins tea in hand.

"There you go H, one sugar."

"Thanks."

They walk across the hive of inactivity that doubles as the breakfast lounge and join Gus.

"All set?"

Gus puts his cup down.

"Yeah, all set. What time do you want to leave?"

"As soon as I've finished my tea. Ok?"

"Cool, I'll go and get my stuff. Meet you by the Volvo."

Gus stands and walks away.

Olivia walks to the table. She hands Gilbert his Bisoprolol which he swallows immediately.

"Need to keep my blood pressure under control today."

Olivia leans closer.

"Almost done. See you at the car in ten minutes?"

"Perfect."

Olivia strolls off. H finishes his tea.

"Right, here we go then."

They all stand and set off on their tasks.

———————————————

Inside the Volvo, Gus, H and Olivia watch the countryside roll by as Shoreham approaches. H turns to Gus and outlines the plan.

"I'll park up where we stopped last time. You and Olivia can stroll over to the hangar and get everything ready. Do you need me?"

"No, I can open the hangar and organise the slot for taking off. We can taxi out easily and then we're off. We'll fly round for about an hour and then land at Redhill Aerodrome. I've booked a landing spot at two o'clock."

"Good work Gus, I'll drive as soon as you are settled and meet you there."

H turns into the slip road and heads for his parking space. He pulls up next to an old Rover and parks. Gus and Olivia step out and head for the hangar, Gus playing with the key to the lock as they walk.

H slides down in the old leather seat and watches as they open the hangar door and fifteen minutes later a bright white small plane noses out from the hangar and taxis a few yards. An overalled grease-covered spotty youth wipes his hands on a rag and pulls the door shut he walks over and does the same on the other side. Gus' arm pokes out of the window waving his thanks and the small plane inches forward and then turns away down the runway. Just moments later the wheels pick up speed and Gus and Olivia hurtle down the tarmac and the Pilatus lifts smoothly into the air.

H finally exhales and realizes he had been holding his breath for a few minutes.

He turns the ignition and sets off for Redhill.

Barely and hour later and H pulls into the small airfield at Redhill. Grass runways and wind sockets. He notices a small white Pilatus standing in front of a large old hangar and heads round the perimeter towards it. Once there he sees Gus and Olivia standing by the plane smiling.

Olivia is almost bouncing up and down.

"That was so great. It's such a rush being in a little plane, Gus is so cool."

"Well done Gus, great work. Let's get this baby inside and start work on the papering."

H walks to the back of the Volvo and heaves two large rolls of sticky-backed white paper and walks into the old hangar.

Gus climbs back in the cockpit and calls for H and Olivia to stand clear; he slowly rolls the plane into the hangar and out of public sight. H closes the hangar doors behind them and Gus hits the brakes and turns the engine off.

He climbs down to the ground and they start work.

Gus and H hold the white sheet up against the registration number and Olivia makes a mark on the paper to show her where to cut. They do this on both sides of the plane and then stick the paper over the registration number. Standing back H admires their handiwork.

"Not bad, not bad at all."

Gus and Olivia concur.

"Once Gil gets to work painting the new reg number it will look fine."

H walks round smoothing the paper with his hand. Close up you can tell but from two hundred yards away you'd never know.

"Right, let's tidy up and get out of here."

Gus and Olivia help tidy the hangar and they leave, locking the hangar behind them using the code Gus has been given. They all get into the Volvo and head for home.

CHAPTER TWENTY TWO – MAGS

The next few days at SummerVale drag by with an interminable slowness. The training has been a morning routine for everyone and they have been joined by another six SummerVale inmates (who have no idea what's going on but just wanted to be alive again). Gus leads the fitness routine and it is a welcome distraction as they all wait as the days tick by.

Mags is preparing herself for the biggest event of her life. She is sitting in her room when Trisha comes in, no knock or pre-able, just a twist of the handle and in.

"Oh just come on in why don't you. Don't worry about my privacy."

Trisha looks at her as you would a small child.

"And what would you be doing in the middle of the morning that anyone would want to see?"

"You never know. The new me might have lots on."

"Of course, let George Clooney out of the wardrobe, he needs to go home and get some rest."

Mags smiles.

"Now that **would** be worth getting caught out for!"

Trisha sits on the side of the bed next to Mags.

"Right, you all packed?"

"Nearly done. Don't like those dungarees though."

"Got to look the part love."

"But the flat shoes make me look about five foot nothing."

"Well that's because you *are* five foot nothing."

"Sod off, my **love**."

Trisha picks up Mags' bag from the bed and weighs it.

"Not too heavy. Where's your new passport?"

"In my handbag."

"Money?"

"Handbag."

"Ticket."

"Bag."

Trisha pauses. Mags chips in.

"Knickers?"

"Bag."

Both old friends burst into laughter. At that moment there is a knock on the door.

Trisha stands to go to the door. Mags goes to stand and winces as she feels a pain in her chest. She rubs it and flexes her shoulders. All seems fine. She turns as Trisha opens the door and H stands in the doorway.

"Ladies, your carriage awaits."

Trisha inches out of the door.

"Just get my bag, won't be a sec."

She squeezes past H and they lock eyes once again.

H steps inside and smiles at Mags.

"Ready?"

Mags takes a deep breath and raises her eyebrows.

"Yes. Ready, willing and able."

"Let's get going. Gatwick is a nightmare sometimes."

H picks up her bag from the bed and heads out of the door.

In the back of H's old Volvo the two soon to be conspirators sit in silence as H heads for Gatwick.

He talks to them over his shoulder.

"Right, so you're all prepped, tickets, passports, money, directions to hotel and directions to the airport?"

Trisha responds for both of them.

"For the sixth time, yes, we are all prepared. Don't worry, we have everything in hand."

"Sorry, just a bit nervous."

Mags, sitting with her right hand rubbing her left hand answers.

"Yes well, we are nervous too. But it will all be fine."

"And Trish, you are ready with the story when Mags goes into her Bette Davis act."

"Yep, all ready, list of the right questions and things to say. We'll be fine."

"Cool. Here we are. North Terminal. I'll stick the car in the short term and come in with you. No dangers here."

The two old ladies say their thanks as H turns into the car park.

As they walk into the check in area, H pushing a trolley with the two bags on it. Trisha and Mags walking just behind him. They walk to check in desk 38 and stand in a short queue. Their turn arrives and they approach the desk together. A young girl at the desk politely asks for their passports and tickets. They hand them over. Mags notices her hand is shaking. The moment of truth, will Costas' fake passports pass muster?

H lifts the bags onto the weigh counter beside the orange faced check-in girl.

"Just the two of you flying?"

H answers quickly.

"Yes, I'm just their chauffeur."

She smiles as H steps away.

"Lugano?"

Trisha steps forward.

"Yes, that's right."

"Did you pack the bag yourself?"

Trisha answers.

"Yes."

"Are you carrying any flammable liquids?"

"No."

"Could anyone have put anything in your bags or has anyone asked you to carry anything?"

"No."

She holds out two boarding cards.

"Miss Stein?"

Mags stands stock still. She doesn't move.

"Miss Stein?"

Mags realises that she is talking to her. She takes the boarding card and her passport.

"Oh thank you, sorry I was thinking of the mountains."

"Have a nice flight."

"Thank you."

"Miss Sappho."

She hands the other boarding card and passport to Trisha.

"Thank you."

"Have a nice flight."

Trisha and Mags turn and walk away, H steps into line with them. Under her breath the check-in girl sums up her feelings.

"Silly old dykes."

They follow the airport signs to the departure gate. As they get there Mags turns to H.

"Don't worry, we'll be fine. It's a good plan, we won't cock it up."

She leans forward and gives him a hug.

Trisha just smiles at him, he goes to say something but she interrupts him with a kiss and a hug and says.

"I know, me too."

She turns and heads for the Departure lounge never looking back. As they disappear beyond the screen H heads back to his car and SummerVale.

The in flight safety presentation is straightforward and soon the trolley dollies are offering food to the passengers.

Mags picks at her chicken korma and rice and Trisha devours her chilli con carne with relish. The flight passes uneventfully and soon Trisha and Mags are in a taxi heading for Hotel Residence Principe Leopoldo. A rural retreat set in a tranquil park. As they pull up Mags puts her hand on Trisha's arm.

"Oh Trish it's so lovely."

They pull up outside and the door is opened by the driver. They pay the fare, just fifteen Euros so Trisha gives him a twenty and tells him to keep the change. He helps them into the hotel with a smile and they check in with a little difficulty as they pay in cash up front rather than put the room on a credit card – primarily as they don't have one in their new names.

Once inside the room they collapse onto the twin beds and lie still for a few minutes then they stand and look out of the window at a beautiful lake.

Trisha soaks up the beauty of the view and squeezes Mags hand.

"Pity we can't just stay here for a couple of weeks, it's gorgeous."

"I know, still, if this works maybe we can do this for real all the time."

"Wouldn't that be lovely."

Trisha gathers herself together.

"Right, a bath then a nice dinner. What do you think?"

"The last supper?"

"The last poor supper maybe."

She walks into the bathroom and turns on the taps and starts to fill her bath.

Early morning and the sun is streaming through the large window. Mags stirs and stretches, she sees Trisha sitting by the window already fully dressed once again in her 'faux lesbian' outfit, a mismatched polka dot top and striped skirt. Mags gets moving and dons her denim dungarees and pulls her hair back in a bun. Trisha picks up her overnight bag.

"Right Gertrude let's roll."

Mags smiles a weak but determined smile.

"Ok...er.......Patricia..."

They walk out of their lovely room and head downstairs. They get a few knowing glances as they stroll through the foyer and the receptionist looks as if she has swallowed a decomposing mouse as she hands them their bill. No extras, just a signature and they ask politely for a taxi to be called.

A mere five minutes later and they are heading back the few kilometres to the airport and the one chance to change their lives.

The check in for the small charter is so much more exclusive and they are hurried through with a minimum of fuss. Hardly any checking and their passports don't even get a second glance.

In the waiting area they sit nervously glancing at the three other passengers waiting by the same gate – a fat German businessman sweating profusely even though it is still early morning and the airport air conditioning is on full blast. A young couple sit close by, smartly dressed and carrying designer bag and briefcase. Trisha looks at the woman and her eyes look at her shoes and thinks they probably cost more than her entire wardrobe back at SummerVale. But not for long.

Mags stands. She leans forward and whispers in Trisha's ear. To the smartly dressed man it looks like she is being overly affectionate in public. His face shows great distaste. Mags says.

"Just need a quick wee."

"Don't be long, I might get lynched."

Mags manages a frail smile and heads for the 'toilette' sign.

Inside she sits in a cubicle as she struggles to catch her breath. A numb feeling in her left hand and a pain in her ribs. She closes her eyes and wills the pain away. She talks herself into feeling better.

"Come on you silly cow, get going."

She takes a deep breath and walks out again.

The airport loudspeaker 'bing – bongs' and their flight is called. They walk to the small gate, show their tickets and they are on the tarmac heading to the small Pilatus standing proudly alone away from the larger planes. Trisha flips her phone and prepares a text for H. As she closes in on the plane she types in the registration number of the plane *N914TZ* and hits send. She exhales quickly and continues to walk to the plane. They reach the short steps and a leggy stewardess offers to assist them in, they decline. They take the seats allocated, comfy leather seats with lots of leg-room. Trisha wiggles as she sits down. She turns to Mags and says *sotto voce*:

"I could so get used to this."

Mags just looks out of the window.

The plane starts its engines and the stewardess checks everyone is strapped in. Trisha has her phone in her hand as she hasn't had a confirmation text back from H. She is sweating and really worried.

"I'm afraid you'll have to turn your phone off now madam."

"In a moment."

The stewardess, used to dealing with rich and pushy clients smiles with a mouth full of perfectly white teeth.

"No madam, you must turn it off now."

Trisha is about to raise another objection when the signal that a message has arrived pings into her phone. Ignoring the leggy blonde in front of her she flips her phone and reads the message.

NIBE ONE TISHA, GOD LUCK

She closes her phone and turns it off. The stewardess just smiles. Trisha turns to Mags.

"He can't text for toffee."

No reply from Mags.

"Here we go, you ready?"

Mags turns and nods. In the light of the cabin Trisha can't see the grey pallor of her old friend. Mags hand grips her chest as the plane begins its journey. The plane taxis out to the runway and immediately rolls forward and accelerates off down the tarmac and swoops into the crisp Swiss air.

CHAPTER TWENTY THREE – THE JOB

Hand the team are sitting round a small table in the ancient hangar that contains their plane. The plane has no registration number just a large white space waiting for the number to be painted on. Gilbert waits, brush in hand, like Van Gogh waiting to start his next masterpiece. The phone beeps. H writes down the plane registration and speaks out loud.

"*N....9....1.....4....T......Z....*"

He types a message back quickly and shuts his phone.

Gus pulls on his uniform jacket and pulls his jacket close.

"Nice one Top Gun."

Olivia removes her coat to reveal her stewardesses outfit. She does a small curtsey.

"Tea, coffee………..me?"

They all laugh. Gilbert stops in mid-stroke.

"Oi, pack it in or we'll have a smudged number."

Gilbert copies the style of registration number he has a photo of and stands back and admires his work.

"Fine."

He skips round the other side and starts there. Just a few minutes later the plane is fully prepared.

H looks at his watch; he has a clipboard in hand and a timetable to follow.

"Right. Off you go."

He looks at Gus who walks over and gives him a hug. Gus hugs Gilbert and climbs into the cockpit and turns the key, the engine fires up and the propeller bursts into life, loud and vibrant. Olivia waves from inside and H and Gilbert pull the doors back. Gus inches the small plane onto the grass runway, pulls back the throttle and the plane rushes away and then swoops into the air.

H and Gilbert close and lock the hangar then climb into the Volvo and head for SummerVale.

On the real plane Trisha and Mags are sitting very still. Knuckles white as they grip the seat rests. Mags is in the window seat and is just staring out. Trisha nudges her.

"Ok hon, you're on."

Mags doesn't reply.

Trisha nudges her again, harder.

No movement.

Trisha reaches over and touches Mags hand to get her to respond. It is cold to the touch. Very cold. Trisha reaches over and touches Mags face. Ice cold.

"Oh my God."

Trisha lets out a wail and calls to the Stewardess.

With a resigned sigh the blonde puts on the smile and wiggles to Trisha's seat.

"How can I help madam?"

Trisha catches her breath as she tries to explain.

"My…err….friend…she's…err…..she's not well."

The stewardess leans across to Mags and gently touches her shoulder.

"Madam…….madam…"

No response.

She reaches down and unbuckles Trisha's seat belt.

"Can I just squeeze in there?"

Trisha moves quickly out of the way.

The stewardess sits in Trisha's seat and leans over Mags.

She looks at her closely. Feels for a pulse. Nothing. She opens an eyelid. Nothing.

She draws in a deep breath.

She turns to Trisha.

"I'm really sorry, your friend seems to have had a heart attack or something. I need to talk to the Captain, excuse me."

She extricates herself from the seat and scurries up to the cabin leaving Trisha standing in the centre of the plane not knowing what to do.

The Captain in his crisp white shirt comes to their seats very sharply. He smiles weakly at Trisha and sits in her seat next to Mags. He feels for a pulse and checks her eyes. He turns to Trisha.

"Oh dear, I'm so sorry. Your friend has passed away. Did she have a history of heart trouble?"

Trisha replies automatically.

"Not that I know of."

The stewardess hands Trisha a handkerchief. Trisha looks at her sideways.

"What?"

"Your face. You're crying."

Trisha takes the handkerchief and wipes away the tears.

The Captain stands and puts a consoling hand on Trisha's arm.

"I'm so sorry. We'll get a Doctor to be standing by at Shoreham."

Trisha suddenly remembers why they are here. What's supposed to happen.

"What?"

"I will arrange for a Doctor and a Coroner to meet us at Shoreham."

"What? We're not going to land now?"

"There's not a lot of point I'm afraid. She's gone and even if we landed at the nearest airport we can't do anything for her. Best to get to Shoreham and sort everything there."

Trisha starts to protest and the Captain is gone. The blonde stewardess motions for her to sit down and takes charge.

"I'll get a blanket to put over her. We have no spare seats so I can't move you I'm afraid. Do you want a cup of tea?"

Trisha's mind is whirling and she nods to the offer of tea as much to get rid of the blonde as actually wanting a tea.

H and Gilbert roar into the courtyard at SummerVale and Gilbert almost leaps out of the car and heads down the lawn to get the van from its hiding place behind the greenhouse.

H trots into SummerVale and heads for George's room. He opens the door and George is sitting at his makeshift desk using the bed as his chair. George is merrily hacking his way into the airport site.

"Been in twice so far. Manifesto reads three crates. All good. No changes to registration. No extra security passwords. Only one plane landing even close to ours and that is five minutes after us, perfect timing to distract the security, the tower and any onlookers."

"Great stuff George. So what do we do now?"

"Absolutely nothing. I will intercept any communication and basically delete it. They will think all is ok and the plane is on schedule."

H exhales loudly and paces up and down.

"This will bloody kill me you know."

"Calm thyself. It's all in hand. Clockwork, sheer clockwork."

"Ok, me and Gilbert are off to the barn. Bring the Volvo when you're done."

H tosses the Volvo keys onto the bed and turns to leave.

"Call me if anything changes."

George just waves an arm in the air ushering H out of the door.

Gus turns the controls slightly to the left and he feels the plane respond immediately, he swoops a little and then brings the nose up. Olivia is sitting next to him and gasps in happiness as the small plane weaves through the sky. She looks at her watch, taps it and leans closer to Gus.

"Twenty minutes, how long to get there?"

Gus checks the altimeter, the speedometer, and his route.

"Fifteen minutes tops, I'll ease off a bit. I hope George has taken care of any other incoming traffic."

Olivia looks behind. The space all set for the cargo and just a small box with Gus' flask of tea sitting on a spare seat.

Gus turns the plane and heads for Shoreham.

Trisha feels very surreal, sitting in a plane next to her dead friend knowing the job now depends on her completely. She is completely lost. What to do. She leans over and touches Mags cheek.

"Ok Mags, my turn."

She loosens her collar in a very dramatic fashion, shifts in her seat, and breathes heavily, loudly. The blonde stewardess totters over to her.

"Are you ok madam?"

Trisha breathes even harder. Almost forcing herself to sweat. She grabs the stewardess's hand and grips it so tight that the stewardess squeals in pain.

She realises that Trisha is in trouble.

"Oh God no......help........stay calm."

She jumps up and goes to talk to the Captain.

In his ear she updates him.

"Oh shit, now the other old dyke is having a fit. I think she is having a heart attack."

"Oh bugger. Let me see."

He jumps out of his seat and the co-pilot takes charge. He walks to Trisha's seat and looks at her. Trisha is grabbing her chest.

"Are.....you.....in......pain?"

As if slowing down his words will make it easier to understand he looks closely at Trisha. She nods.

"My......chest......it hurts....."

"Oh God, she's having a heart attack. Probably stress due to her friend popping her clogs."

The stewardess looks at him.

"What do we do?"

"Try and land somewhere quick."

The Captain goes back to his seat.

"Where's the nearest airport?"

His young co-pilot plots their course, checks his chart.

"Auxerre, five minutes."

"Right, contact them; tell them we have a fatality on board and an old lady having a heart attack. Get them to prepare an ambulance and a coroner. If the French have such a thing? Suzy, check her passport, get her details, age, contact if possible."

Suzy, the blonde trolley dolly goes off to search Trisha's bags and returns with a passport.

"Patricia Sappho, born 1945. That makes her.......erm........"

"Sixty three."

"I would have got there."

"Right, go stay with her, let her know help is coming and don't let her die."

"How do I do that?"

"Give her the kiss of life if you need to."

"Yuk...........no way, who knows where her mouth has been."

She leaves.

The captain turns to his co-pilot.

"Like she's never had her mouth anywhere nasty."

The co-pilot just grins.

"Right, let Shoreham know we'll be late, just so we can carry on later."

The co-pilot starts to send a message which will end up in email form on the Shoreham screens.

Gilbert pulls up the van behind the barn off the road and out of sight. H jumps out and walks round the front. He peers round the corner. Nothing in sight. Big sigh of relief. Gilbert joins him and they undo the chain securing the doors and pull them open. The large empty barn stares back at them.

H looks at his old pal.

"Just have to wait and hope nothing goes wrong."

"How long?"

"Maybe an hour, maybe a bit more."

Gilbert sits on the floor with his back to the barn and removes a roll-up from behind his ear and lights it sending a plume of smoke up above his head.

George sees the email from **N914TZ.** He looks at it, then rubs his eyes and looks again.

SHOREHAM TOWER. FORCED TO LAND AT AUXERRE. ONE FATALITY ONE HEART ATTACK. WILL BE ARRIVING MINIMUM OF TWO HOURS LATE. WILL ADVISE WHEN CLOSER.

CAPTAIN J VEASEY

George copies the email, saves it then deletes it. He picks up his mobile phone and hovers over the keys. What to say?

Gus closes in on Shoreham and makes contact with the tower.

"Tower this is N for November…niner, one, four, T for Tango…Z for Zulu permission to land. Over."

The tower crackles into life.

"No problems, you're right on time. Have you done this run before?"

"Negative tower, first time. Captain Weeks here. Where's the pick – up point?"

"On the left, see the yellow marker. Three crates and two passengers to pick up."

Gus and Olivia exchange glances of alarm. Passengers! They haven't prepared for this.

Gus flicks off the radio.

"Oh shit."

Olivia heads for the back of the plane.

"Right, no panic, I'll think of something."

"Well do it quick, we're landing. Get strapped in."

Inside the tower, Charlie Stephens holds his binoculars up to his eyes. He picks out the Pilatus and checks the registration, reading the code out loud.

Satisfied he lowers the binoculars and sits down.

Gus turns the plane and lines it up with the small runway and lowers the nose, eases back on the throttle and gently touches down, a beautiful landing.

The radio crackles again.

"Nice landing Captain Weeks, you can see Gerry with the blocks over to your right. Taxi there. We have another incoming in ten minutes; hold tight and we'll get you away on time."

"Thanks. I see him."

Gus can see a boiler-suited youth waving his arms and carrying wheel blocks. Gus rolls to a stop and the youth rams the wheel blocks in place.

Gus switches off the engine. Olivia gets out of her seat and opens the door.

The same youth is now rolling towards them driving the steps. He lines them up and attaches them to the door opening. Olivia works her way down and opens the cargo hatch. Olivia moves forward and steps out of the plane, she spots two brightly clad pensioners standing some hundred yards away. She realises they are her passengers so she waves politely and puts her hand up to motion for them to stay where they are. A rumble and a small forklift truck carrying a large crate being driven by the same youth is heading to the cargo hold. He drops the crate gently into the interior of the plane and shoots off to pick up the next one.

Inside the tower Charlie Stephens focuses his binoculars on Olivia.

"Bloody hell, these private charter dollies are so fit. No lard arse long haul grannies for them. Lucky buggers. She's scrummy."

"Put those down you perv, incoming in four minutes."

"Spoilsport."

The second crate is loaded and the third is on its way. The two passengers are just standing watching this all play out.

The third crate is loaded and the driver parks his forklift and walks to the steps.

"Three items loaded as per manifest. Just Mr and Mrs Kowalski to board."

Olivia gives him her best teeth and tits look and almost flutters her eyelids.

"I'll just go and have a word with them."

She strides down the steps and heads for the old couple.

"Hello, Mr and Mrs Kowalski?"

The two jazzily dressed, tubby would be passengers pick up small cases and smile.

Olivia disarms them with her smile.

"We have to let you know this by law, but don't worry."

The old lady is a little worried already. In a broad Southern American accent she half answers, half questions both Olivia and her husband.

"Let us know what? Arthur, ask her, go on."

"Ok Marge, let her speak."

Olivia keeps the smile in place.

"Well, part of our manifest today, you know, the cargo, is a phial of bacterial test tubes. The flask containing these phials must be delivered to a laboratory in Switzerland today so we will need you to sign a release form. It's just a precaution."

"Against what?"

"Well, even though the phials are safe the contents are very dangerous if mixed with the atmosphere and inhaled. I'll just get the form."

Olivia turns to go back to the plane.

"Excuse me young lady."

Olivia turns hiding her smile.

"We'll wait for the next flight if that's okay. We're in no hurry we're on holiday. We've treated ourselves to a tour of Europe. Our next stop is Austria for a coach tour that starts on Saturday so we have plenty of time don't we Arthur."

Arthur just nods.

"Well if you're sure. Tell you what. As a gesture, the airline will refund fifty percent of your ticket price when you arrive in Lugano. How's that sound?"

"Oh my, that's so generous. Thank you so much."

"You can go and relax back at the departure lounge; there will be another flight this afternoon."

"Well that's fine then, isn't it Arthur."

Arthur just nods.

Olivia turns and walks up the steps. The spotty youth sneaks a sly look at her legs as she walks up.

She closes the door and the youth removes the steps.

Olivia grins at Gus.

"Let's get the fuck outta here."

"Yes ma'am."

The propellers thunder into life and Gus inches the plane onto the centre of the runway in keeping with the towers instructions. He gets clearance and roars down the tarmac and pulls the plane into the Sussex air. He let's out a whoop of delight as they watch the small airfield disappear below them.

In Auxerre the plane taxis to a remote part of the airport and a French ambulance pulls up alongside the plane and Trisha is loaded onto a gurney and then into the ambulance. The doors are quickly shut and she lies on her back, oxygen mask on her mouth listening as they discuss her condition in French. They are surprised that her heart rate is fine and her blood pressure normal.

Behind her Mags body is loaded into the coroner's wagon and taken off for examination.

CHAPTER TWENTY FOUR - ESCAPE

Almost immediately the small Pilatus has pulled up over the outbuildings and cleared the airspace around the airport Gus turns right and heads inland. He punches in the field co-ordinates and switches off the radio.

"Don't need anyone scanning our frequency from here on."

They head for Morrissey's Farm and the details dictate that Gus has seven minutes of flying time only. He brings the plane lower to stay clear of the airspace of any larger aeroplanes coming in to land.

Gus lowers the flaps and prepares to land. He shouts over his shoulder.

"Olivia, strap yourself in, this could get a bit bumpy."

Olivia takes her seat just behind Gus, her uniform making a rustling sound as she straps herself in.

"Here we go."

Gus looks out at a small hedgerow that grows larger every second. The large poplar trees at the far end of the field suddenly changing from a small hedge to a large line of trees very, very quickly. The trees now fill Gus' vision. He slows the plane a touch as they swoop ever closer. Olivia looks out over Gus' shoulder and sees the trees coming up fast.

"Oh Jesus."

She can't help uttering something as the landing has always been on her mind.

The wheels of the small plane brush the tops of the trees as they swoop down towards the green expanse of field. As the leaves scrape along the base of the plane Olivia can't contain herself.

"Ohhhh shiiiiiiiit."

Gus grips the controls and checks all his angles. The wheels are close to the ground and they are still moving at quite a rate. The wheels touch the ground with a bump, too fast, the plane jumps back into the air and the barn at the far end of the field seems to leap forward at them. Gus lowers the plane once more and the wheels touch down again, a small bounce and they are racing across the ground, not in the air at least.

Still moving way too fast, the barn now fills the whole of Gus and Olivia's perspective.

H, Gilbert and George (who have just pulled up in the Volvo and the van) watch the small plane swoop over the trees. Gilbert whoops with delight.

"Fuck me sideways with a chainsaw they've made it."

The three men link arms, cuddle and shout at the top of their voices, they dance around like whirling dervishes and scream in delight. H breaks away and shouts at them to get the barn doors open quickly.

George and Gilbert run to the centre of the barn, grab a door each and ease them open until the gaping door of the barn is wide open awaiting the fast approaching plane. H looks, the plane is approaching fast, way too fast for his liking. Gus is running out of field.

Inside the plane Gus is standing on the brakes, smoke starts to come off the rubber and the squeal of brakes seem very loud as the barn grows ever bigger and closer. Gus shouts at Olivia, screaming to be heard above the screech of the engine and the brakes.

"Grab hold of something and pray."

Olivia's eyes are bulging with fright. She can see H, George and Gilbert waving at them frantically.

She screams.

"Fuuuuccckkk."

H waves at the plane as if by doing this he can slow it down. Just a mere fifty yards away. H's mind is in turmoil. He starts to try and work out how far it is in metres, he shakes his head to make himself think sensibly. He can't.

The plane's wheels are smoking.

The squeal of brakes on tyres fills the air. George turns away and crouches down. Gilbert heads for the safety of the trees next to the barn.

Gus fights to keep the plane straight and the wheels from locking. He pumps the brakes as his knuckles turn white with the effort. The barn is almost on him and the plane is still moving quickly. He is almost out of his seat jamming his feet on the brakes as the plane slows. He sees H just to the side as the plane cruises past.

The earth under the wheels creates a large dust cloud behind and covers H and George in a brown coating as the wings of the plane roll past the framework of the barn doors and the wheels finally grind to a halt five yards inside the empty barn.

He puts the lock on and flexes his hands. He laughs as he says out loud.

"Ladies and gentlemen, welcome to The Barn."

He turns to look at Olivia who is as white as a ghost.

"Same time next week Miss Phipps?"

Olivia bursts into laughter and throws her arms around him and gives him as much of a squeeze as the seatbelt will allow.

"Well done Gus, well done."

Gus inches the plane fully into the barn

Gus switches off the engine. He undoes his seat belt and stands up. The effort and pressure has really got to him and he wobbles a bit and grabs hold of his seat and holds on tight. Olivia notices this and looks at him closely.

She adopts a Wallace and Gromit voice, mocking his Yorkshire roots.

"Eeeeh Gromit, a reet close shave."

"Ay lass, too bloody close."

Suddenly there is a banging on the door from the outside. Olivia gets out of her seatbelt and walks unsteadily back. She opens the door and looks out on H, George and a puffing Gilbert, all smiling but concerned.

George grins up at them.

"Nothing like a precision landing Gus. A bit squeaky bum time though."

Gus peeps over Olivia's shoulder.

"Can I have a brown uniform next time please?"

H offers his hand to help Olivia down from the plane. He then does the same for Gus. They hug.

"Thanks Gus, that was amazing."

"No problem. Never worried……..much."

H rolls his eyes. He turns to Gilbert.

"Gil, bring the van round, let's get loaded and bugger off."

Gilbert sets off round the side of the barn, reaching for the van keys as he trots along.

H looks up at the cargo.

"Three crates, excellent. Any problems?"

Olivia pulls a face.

"Not really, just two old Americans with tickets back to Switzerland, so, no real problems."

"What did you do? Are they in the plane?"

"Oh yeah, we tied them up and chucked them in the back."

"So what ***did*** you do?"

"I told them they were welcome to fly to Switzerland with us but they would need to sign the warranty form to allow them to travel with chemicals that might be unstable and that the consent form also contains a release from the airline should anything happen to them or they catch anything nasty."

H looks at Olivia in awe.

"And they bought it?"

"They said they would get a later flight."

"Blimey, good thinking Olivia."

Gilbert drives up in his white van, doors open. He parks side on to allow easy access. George climbs into the Pilatus crowbar in hand and sets to work on the lid of the nearest crate.

Too heavy to move while full, the contents need to be transported to the van. A cracking sound, the wooden crate splinters and George removes the lid. He starts to pass the items down to H and Gus who together with Gilbert and Olivia form a human chain to move the contents quickly.

Less than fifteen minutes later and all three crates have been emptied, contents removed, crates loaded onto the van and crates refilled.

The three crates fill the back of the white van.

H turns to Gilbert.

"You and Gus get going; we'll lock up and tidy up here. We'll doctor the plane a bit, remove the registration number and clean up then we'll be with you. Got the Volvo keys?"

George throws them casually to H and heads for the van.

"Okay."

Gilbert and Gus climb into the van, shut the doors and with a casual wave set off for the gate halfway down the large field. H's phone beeps advising him that he has a text message. He reads it and stands very still for a minute.

The text is from Trisha. It is straight to the point.

Mags dead. Heart attack. Very sad. I'm in hospital but ok. Don't worry. Home soonest. T x

His head drops and he shakes it from side to side gently. Olivia notices this and calls over to him.

"Everything alright?"

He composes himself before replying.

"Yes, just another bill being chased. Let's crack on."

Olivia looks hard at him; she doesn't believe him but lets it go.

Olivia and George have already started to rub down the surfaces of the plane when H turns away from the field. H rips the paper sheet from the side of the plane revealing the true registration beneath. He rolls up the large paper sheet and then walks round the other side and repeats the action. A whole new plane now stands in front of them. George rubs down the sides with a cloth. Satisfied he walks to the van and dumps the screwed up paper in the foot well. George climbs into the front seat of the van and leans back against the seat with a large sigh. H walks over and slides the left hand door shut and loops the chain through the handle. H calls up to the other two.

"How we doing? Ready to go soon?"

George pokes his head out of the open hold.

"Almost, just making sure no prints are left. Just in case."

"Ok fella. Let's hurry on in case some nosy sod has called the old bill."

Olivia jumps down from the plane shortly followed by George.

They follow H out of the barn, pull the other door shut and pull the chain through the handle. H clicks the padlock in place and with a flourish George wipes it with his trusty duster. They all set off round the back of the barn and climb into the Volvo, much bigger than Olivia's cute little Nissan. She turns the key and the engine throbs into life.

"SummerVale here we come."

With a whoop and a cheer she sets off.

She looks at H and catches his eye. He looks troubled. She turns onto the road and they head for the safety of SummerVale's walls.

CHAPTER TWENTY FIVE – SUMMERVALE

They turn into the driveway at SummerVale and all three of them are looking out for police cars. None are around. So far so good. The van is nowhere to be seen, which is a good thing…… or a bad thing. Olivia is looking everywhere and then catches sight of Gilbert at the window of SummerVale, a cup of tea in hand and she relaxes.

They go into the lounge and everyone gets together. They get a few strange looks as they hug each other and jig around. Mrs Hailsham comes in to prepare for the evenings bingo. Olivia comes in having changed back into her nurse's outfit. She breaks away from the group just in time and makes out she is talking to another older inmate that is actually asleep.

Gilbert talks to H out of the side of his mouth.

"The van is behind the greenhouse. We can check it out later."

"Why are you talking like a stroke victim? I think we'll wait for a week or so before touching anything. See if anything shows up on the news. Besides, I think we should wait until Trisha gets back."

Gilbert nods in agreement.

"Ok."

Gus sneaks upstairs to take his uniform off; George can't stop smiling and decides to take a walk to cool his mind. One by one H talks to them all and tells everyone to have a siesta then come back down for bingo. They all agree and bounce off in their own way to try and calm down.

Early evening in the SummerVale lounge and the 'team' of H, Gus, George, Gilbert and Olivia sit at a corner table as the weekly bingo gets into full swing.

They distractedly cross out numbers as they are called. In the background of his mind H can barely hear the calls.

"All the fours, forty four. Two fat ladies, eighty eight. On its own, number one."

In an instant George let's out a yelp.

"House"

He stands and walks with his card to the desk. The metal cage containing the balls is now still as Eric the Bingo checks George's card. Satisfied he has won he hands over a twenty pound note.

"Lucky boy George. What are you going to buy with your winnings?"

George looks at him in quiet disdain (after all there is a huge pile of cash waiting for him behind the greenhouse……. he hopes) and replies.

"New socks."

He turns on his heel and walks back to the table pocketing the twenty pound note as he goes. H stops him before he can sit down.

"Let's get a drink for everyone. Give me a hand."

They walk to the makeshift bar and get a round in. They carry the drinks back on a tray. George places the tray on the table and they all take their drink. George and H sit down.

H motions with his fingers for everyone to come forward, they all lean in.

"I have some really bad news I'm afraid. I don't have any details but Trisha texted me, Mags has died."

His words hang in the air. Olivia gasps and puts her hand to her mouth as her eyes well up. The others all sit in silence. Gus breaks the silence.

"How?"

H continues.

"Trisha's text just said heart attack. Maybe the strain of it all was too much."

"Yeah, maybe."

George chips in.

"The Captain just said one fatality and one heart attack. Nothing more."

George and H had already discussed how to break the news and they decided to keep it brief.

"We'll find out more when Trisha gets back but until then we can't let on that we know anything. It's even more important that we leave the van hidden for a while. Let's decide what to do when we're all together."

H picks up his drink. He raises it to the middle of the group.

"To Mags."

They all join in and clink their glasses together with a collective "Mags".

They finish the bingo in near silence all lost in their own thoughts.

As Eric the Bingo wraps up the evening they all drift off to bed. The euphoria of the job, escaping, and the excitement of what they have achieved is all put into perspective by the loss of their friend.

They arrange to meet the following morning and Gus manages a solitary smile as he says goodnight. Olivia heads outside and walks with H to her car.

"I feel terrible. I wonder what happened?"

"We'll find out when Trisha gets back. I don't want to call just in case. She kept her text short so I don't know what's going on. It's a bloody nightmare."

"It's not your fault H, don't blame yourself. We all entered into this with full knowledge of what might happen."

"Yes, getting arrested was a possibility, not dying."

Olivia places a hand on his arm.

"Call me if you hear anything at any time. Ok?"

"Yes, get some rest. See you in the morning."

Olivia climbs into her little car and drives off. H stands and watches as she exits the large gateway. He puts his hands in his pockets and walks slowly to the door.

CHAPTER TWENTY SIX - MR WATTS

"What?"

A scream from Lord Hunter – Brown.

"How can this happen you useless, incompetent moron."

He is starting to turn purple.

"Fuck, fuck, fuck, fuck, fuck, fuck…….fuck."

The air is silent after his rant.

"I need that crate back in one piece."

A pause as Roland tries to think of a way to explain the reasons for him not being able to get the crate back.

"You ignorant, moronic, low life little shit stain, *I NEED THAT CRATE* BACK. Do you understand?"

Spluttering from the other end of the phone.

"Don't splutter you horrid little man. How do I get my possessions back?"

A pause again as Roland tries to explain.

"I'm sorry your Lordship, nothing I can do. We handed the crate to the airport authorities they took charge, signed the paperwork and that was all I ever do."

"Then what happened?"

"The plane landed and they loaded the crates and the plane took off."

"Yes, then what?"

"Well, two hours later the same plane landed and the crates were obviously not there."

"How did the same plane land twice?"

"Well, it seems the first plane might have been a ringer."

"What?"

"A ringer, not what it seems."

"You mean someone has stolen my crate?"

"Well……………..yes."

"So what do I do now?"

Roland coughs on the other end of the line.

"Call the cops?"

"Ha bloody ha, you know I can't do that. I need someone to find my crate discreetly, quietly, and quickly."

"Well, there is a bloke I know in Watford who is a specialist. He's not cheap but very good."

"Give me his name and details"

Lord Hunter-Brown takes a very expensive fountain pen from his blazer pocket and poises it over the writing pad on his desk.

Roland, obviously looking up the number says a few muffled words through his chin as the phone is wedged under it as he searches.

Success.

"Yes, here it is. Got a pen?"

"Of course you silly little man."

"His name is Oliver Watts, his number is 01923 600007."

Lord Hunter-Brown scribbles the name and number down.

"007?"

"Yes, like James Bond."

"Right."

He puts the phone down. Roland being no use to him anymore. He didn't hear Roland finish his end of the conversation with a resounding "Wanker."

The phone in Oliver Watts' dishevelled office rings loudly in the silence. Oliver reaches over and lifts the receiver.

"Watt You Want Investigations, Oliver Watts speaking, how can I help?"

Lord Hunter – Brown inches his chair forward and rests his elbow on the large desk.

"Hello, yes. Erm…. My name is Lord Hunter – Brown, I understand you specialise in finding lost items?"

"It's one of our services. What have you lost?"

"It's a bit delicate. Could you meet me tomorrow to discuss?"

Oliver Watts fiddles with his diary. He opens it to the correct day. Blank pages stare back at him.

"I'll check my diary."

He rustles the paper a bit.

"I'm free tomorrow morning. Is that any good?"

"Yes that's fine. Meet me at my house in Mayfair."

"Ok, can you give me the address?"

He picks up a cheap biro and scribbles the address down.

"See you at say ten o'clock?"

"Nine. I need you to get to work on this."

Oliver is about to respond when the buzzing of the phone tells him the other party has hung up.

"Well up yours too."

He replaces the receiver and leans back in his chair. Some much needed work and a chance to get back on his feet a bit. He's happy.

The morning is already warming up as Oliver sits outside the imposing town house in a very salubrious part of London. It's ten to nine and he is ready for his meeting with Lord Hunter – Brown; dressed in his best suit and a loud tie he looks every inch the private detective.

He leaves his car, locks it and walks up the immaculate stone steps and rings the bell. The man who answers introduces himself as Lord Hunter – Brown and ushers him in.

Sitting in an ornate study Lord Hunter-Brown sits opposite Oliver and gets straight to the point (no offer of tea or coffee Oliver notes).

"Right, I have some very delicate documents that seem to have been stolen from a plane on its way to my bank in Switzerland. I want them back."

Oliver says nothing, just makes notes. He waits.

"The crate number is 946848. The item I require back is a box wrapped in a purple velvet cover. There are quite a few other items of value in there and a substantial amount of money as well but I really want the box back. It is vitally important."

Oliver clears his throat and looks at his Lordship.

"Can I be candid with you, your Lordship?"

The furrowed brow on Lord Hunter-Browns face tells its own story.

"Of course."

"Well, my questions are many, which airport?"

"Shoreham."

"In Sussex?"

"Yes, get geography GCE did you?"

"I haven't read or heard a robbery being reported. Why is that?"

"Because the people who were robbed do not want it being made public."

"Hmmm."

"How heavy is the box?"

"Light, as I told you already, it only contains documents."

"Are the contents saleable?"

"What?"

"Well, if whoever has taken this crate opens the box will they know the value of the contents? If they saw a bag full of diamonds then they would head for Hatton Garden and sell them. Are the contents valuable on the open market?"

"Not really. The contents are more important to me than anyone else. I am willing to pay for their safe return."

"How much?"

The question hangs in the air.

"One hundred thousand pounds."

This hangs in the air for even longer as Oliver digests what has just been said.

"It must be valuable then."

"It is. I am willing to pay you one hundred thousand pounds for the safe return of the '***unopened***' box. I'll pay your expenses up to two hundred pounds per day plus legitimate out of pocket costs but no fee. This is my final offer."

"Well it seems very acceptable. I need some more info and I'll get cracking."

"Fire away but make it quick."

Oliver looks at his pad. He starts to ask all the pertinent questions he thinks will help lead him to the pot of gold, or in his case, a crate of gold, at the end of the rainbow.

Twenty minutes later he is satisfied he has enough information to start work. He stands and offers his hand. Lord Hunter-Brown ignores the outstretched hand and walks to the door and opens it.

Oliver walks to the door. He looks at the effete upper-class monstrosity holding the door open.

"I'll be in touch."

"You do that."

The door is unceremoniously shut almost catching Oliver's coat – belt as it shuts. He hurries down the steps and heads for his tatty old car and the dream job he is starting to think might cause him major grief.

He whistles as he walks away. The curtains behind him twitch as his Lordship watches the man who can save him walk away.

CHAPTER TWENTY SEVEN – TRAIL

Oliver Watts starts his detective work in his small office on top of Wongs Noodle Bar in Watford. A very strange working environment as the clubs and bars along the High Street rock to the sound of teenage drinkers and fighting males every evening and especially on a Friday and Saturday night. It offers him a very good chance to have a decent office at a very competitive price. He begins his routine as he always does; he leaves the office with his notebook, walks round the corner to Joe's Greasy Spoon and orders a cup of tea and a bacon and runny egg sandwich. He settles in the corner and makes notes using all the information passed on by His Lordship:

PLANE ?

LANDING ?

OTHER PLANE ?

THIEVES ?

CCTV ?

LANDING – WHERE ?
CRATES – CONTENTS ?

He starts to make notes about where he will start to investigate and then his sandwich is placed in front of him. He puts down his pen and immediately bites into the white cholesterol heaven sandwich. He makes an involuntary "Mmmmm" as he tastes the bacon and egg melding together in his mouth.

After finishing his tea and wiping the egg from his chin he makes notes on a second page.

LORD HUNTER - BROWN ?
CRATE ?
CONTENTS ?
NO POLICE - WHY ?
HISTORY ?

He nods his head as if to confirm his list is concise then he stands, pays at the counter and returns to his small, cluttered office.

Sitting at the computer he logs into Google-Earth. He starts by noting any large flat areas close to the airport that a plane might land. Nothing really shows up. He extends his search and after an hour and a radius of 100 miles from the airport (but only in three directions due to the sea being right next to the airport and thinking the small plane didn't skip abroad) he has seventeen potential sights. It's a start.

On his small notebook he has a number for the airport security and makes an appointment for the following day. He calls Auxerre airport in France and with some difficulty makes an appointment for the following week with the head of the airport. He books a return flight to Auxerre on Ryan Air for £30 plus tax. He makes a note of his expenses; he includes his sandwich and tea. Lord

Twitty is paying his daily expenses and all out of pocket costs. His fee will be paid only if he recovers the box His Lordship craves. But, a hundred grand is a hundred grand. Next he hits Google again and types in his employers details and speaks out loud to no-one but himself.

"L.O.R.D. H.U.N.T.E.R. hyphen B.R.O.W.N."

The information highway drives him down a very interesting road for the next two hours. He has a tiger by the tail with this job.

A drive to Shoreham next day and a meeting with Damien Stephens reveals quite a lot of information but no identity clues. A copy of the CCTV footage from the security office costs him £100. He then drives to the first two fields plucked from Google – Earth. No joy at either.

He spends the next two days driving to eight more fields. None reveal anything.

His flight to Auxerre is more revealing; he gets to look at the paperwork for the deceased lady. Her address is listed as SummerVale Retirement Home but she flew under an assumed name on a false passport. Interesting. He gets a copy of the other lady's statement. A Miss Stein. He is getting a bit warmer.

Numerous calls from Lord Hunter – Brown, increasingly abusive calls, don't endear him to his client or help his concentration.

After almost two weeks of investigation and no concrete evidence he believes he needs to visit SummerVale. As he sits at his desk he puts another security tape in the machine. He sees three old guys walking round the airport perimeter, he sees plane spotters, he sees many cars coming and going. What he doesn't see is anything to lead him to the plane and the crates.

He gets in his car and heads for SummerVale. He arrives at an old people's home. He scratches his head. He watches the gate and then drives in and parks so he has a view of the main door. He spends some time doing a sudoku in his paper. The door opens and he glances up as three men emerge, two white and one black. He lifts his camera and clicks a few frames off then quickly lowers the camera and raises the paper.

His brain is starting to buzz. What he's thinking is almost unbelievable.

"Nah. That's insane."

He drives away with a crazy thought running through his head.

Back in his home town he rushes the camera to Boots and prints off the photos he has taken at SummerVale, he compares the photos to the CCTV pictures and makes notes.

"Right, now we are getting somewhere."

Next day he has planned two of his last four field visits and he decides to go to SummerVale afterwards.

He pulls up at the side gate to Morrissey's Farm. He looks over the gate and sees a row of high poplar trees at one end and a barn way off in the distance to his left. He takes a photo, climbs the gate and sets off toward the barn. The net might be closing.

Oliver Watts drives back to SummerVale, he has most of his questions lined up but now they take on a more certain significance. He parks under the lean – to and walks to the main door. It is open, he enters cautiously. He sees a sign for reception and pharmacy. He walks the way the sign says and taps on Olivia's door. He leans his head to the door and hears some papers rustling. The door handle rattles and he jerks his head back and stands up straight. Olivia opens the door to a dishevelled young (ish) man in a scruffy overcoat, a day's stubble but clear blue eyes and a twinkling smile.

"Hello, Miss Phipps?"

"Yes."

"I'm Oliver Watts, I'm trying to get some information for my employer, I wonder if you could spare me a few minutes?"

"I'm really busy this morning….."

"I promise, just a few moments, please."

"Well, make it quick."

She opens the door

"Well you see, Margaret Hornsby, a resident here I believe, died recently on an aeroplane on the way back from Switzerland. She had a false passport on her. She travelled under the name of Stein. She also had her real I.D. on her too. The plane she was on was forced to land in France at a small airport called St. Etienne due to a passenger having a heart attack; one Miss Sappho, who it turns out is really Patricia Kinchin I believe. According to the French Authorities anyway."

He looks at Olivia for confirmation but she stays silent.

"Then another plane landed at the airport and picked up some cargo, including something belonging to my employer. I'm trying to track it down."

Olivia glares back at this smiling assassin.

"What's that got to do with me?"

"Well Miss Phipps, the ground crew and air traffic guys at the airport said there was, and I quote" (He flips a note pad open to read) " a really attractive woman on the plane who was security and air stewardess combined."

Olivia smiles back coldly.

"Well that clearly counts me out then!"

"Oh I don't know, I bet you scrub up quite nicely."

"Charming. Well, I've never been to Shoreham so that's a stretch."

"Not really, I don't remember mentioning which airport it was."

Olivia freezes. She has made a major ricket.

"The paperwork from poor Margaret's return mentioned that she was headed there. That's where I heard the name."

Oliver smiles like a cobra.

"Good save Miss Phipps."

"I really have to make my rounds, if you'll excuse me."

"Is Patricia Kinchin available?"

"She's away on holiday."

"Of course she is. Where?"

"No idea, excuse me."

She walks and opens the door and he starts to leave. As he gets to the door he turns.

"Fancy a coffee sometime? Or dinner?"

She is alarmed. Interrogation then he asks for a date.

"Goodbye."

She closes the door and slumps against the inside.

Back in his car the phone rings, he removes it from his jacket pocket.

"Hello."

Lord Hunter-Brown screams down the phone at him.

"Well? You fuckwit, have you found my property?"

"Not yet but…"

"If I wanted buts I'd have hired a bloody Indian. Stop wheedling and tell me what's going on."

"Well, I think I have a handle on the crates, I'll need a few more days to confirm its whereabouts."

"Well bloody well get on with it, don't waste time talking to me."

The phone goes dead in his hand.

"Tosser."

He double checks that the phone is indeed dead.

He drives back to sunny Watford and starts to scribble some notes in his ever present notepad.

He is now sure of what happened, still can't believe it but deciding what to do next might be the most important decision of his life.

He makes a note to revisit SummerVale later this week. He speaks out loud to no-one.

"Ok guys, time to piss or get off the pot."

He re-writes all the events in chronological order and shakes his head once again.

"Incredible."

The sun has set over the pond in the SummerVale garden when a taxi pulls up and deposits Trisha on the driveway. A small piece of hand-luggage in her hand she looks a frail and forlorn figure. The main door opens and Olivia, H, Gus and Gilbert rush out to greet her. Olivia hugs her and then H closes in, as he gets to her the dam breaks and she sobs uncontrollably for a few minutes with H stroking her hair and trying to calm her.

"Come inside. Let's go somewhere quiet to talk."

They troop upstairs to H's room. Trisha sits on the bed and dabs her eyes with a handkerchief.

"Sorry, silly old sod."

"Forget it. Tell us everything."

Trisha explains exactly what happened and the subsequent spell in a French hospital.

"Luckily I had my E111 card or they would never have taken me into hospital. They were lovely though. I managed to keep all discussions very bland by acting like a dull old biddy. They didn't seem to question my illness. They sent poor Mags back almost straight away."

"Yeah. She is in the local Funeral Parlour. We have arranged a cremation next Wednesday at ten. We had to wait until we knew you were coming back."

"Thank you... It seems such a waste."

"Listen. You get some rest. We'll come by later. Or call if you need anything. "

.Trisha catches H's eye and gives him the briefest weak smile.

They leave to let her get some rest.

CHAPTER TWENTY EIGHT- CONFRONTATION

The sun is only just up as Oliver turns quietly into SummerVale. The tyres on his VW Convertible crunch gently over the gravel. He parks next to H's Volvo and pulls the lever by his chair. The seat reclines and he closes his eyes. He is asleep almost immediately. From his window, H watches, he is not asleep.

After three hours of pacing H decides that affirmative action is the order of the day. He leaves number 68 and walks down to the breakfast room. It's very quiet as he enters, just one other body in a quiet corner. H wonders if she had been there all night or if indeed she was still alive. He is about to go and check when her hand moves and picks up a magazine. He sighs a little sigh of relief and sits down next to the window overlooking the lawn after picking up a cup of tea en route. He is staring out of the window when a voice behind him shakes him out of his reverie. He doesn't jump as he has been waiting for this.

"Mind if I sit down?"

"Take the weight off your notebook Mr Watts. Sit down and have a cuppa."

"Thank you. I will Mister Hitchcock."

A cup is placed on the table opposite H and the rumpled investigator flops down.

"Breakfast with Columbo, I feel privileged. What brings you here at this ungodly hour? As if I don't know. How do you know my name?"

"Well, it's been an interesting ride. I found your name from the register in Miss Phipps office. I have been putting all the pieces of a very complicated jigsaw together. You know you made two mistakes."

He waits for a response but gets none from the ex-lawyer. He flips his constant companion, the notebook and looks at a couple of scribbles.

"Margaret had SummerVale documents in her bag. Very sad."

"So what?"

"Well, that tied her into here."

"You've got to live somewhere. You have a rock that you call home I'm sure, or do you live in that piece of shit Beetle?"

"No, I have a house; just don't use it too much. But bear with me. The other mistake is that airports all have top notch close circuit TV cameras and you and the other.....gentlemen have all been captured scoping the airport."

"There is no law against plane spotting, unless you are in Greece."

"What?"

"Old story."

"Well, I think you and your buddies did a splendid job flying in a bogus plane and nicking the three crates destined for Switzerland. The contents of which the owners didn't want to report."

"So what the hell is your problem?"

"My employer is a very important man, he has some documents …"

H interrupts.

"Had."

"What?"

"He had some important documents. Has would imply that he still has them. He clearly doesn't or you wouldn't be here nosing around."

Oliver smiles, he really likes the chutzpah in this old boy.

"My client *had* some very important documents on that plane, or should I be more accurate, that *should* have been on that plane or the real one anyway. He is mightily pissed. I have been employed to find with said documents no matter what it takes. My nosiness has lead me here. To you. Interesting. Don't you think?"

H finishes his tea. He looks long and hard at Oliver, smiles a resigned smile and takes a deep breath.

"I suppose the evidence that we were plane spotting and that Margaret, rest her lovely soul, was an inmate here proves that we all *might* have a link to this …what…robbery? I haven't read anything in the papers. Was there a robbery?"

"Oh, I know there was, but you and I both know the people you robbed can't tell the police, they just have to suck it up and say nothing. The airline is upset, the airport is embarrassed, the only one with a real gripe is my upper class twit client."

"Really."

"Yes really, and he wants blood."

"Whos?"

"Mine if I don't deliver. So listen. This dodgy flight to Switzerland has been going on for many years now and it's never been rumbled. Until now. You put the two old lezzies on the plane in Switzerland."

"They were just coming back from a short holiday."

"Cobblers, let me finish, please."

"Ok, go ahead."

"The ladies then get the plane to land in France."

"What by dying. That's a bit extreme don't you think?"

"Hear me out please."

"Well don't talk such crap."

Oliver smiles, he has rattled H for the first time.

"Right, so they get the plane to land, it's a very sad addendum that....(he looks at his notepad) Miss Stein, very funny, died on board. Her real name, at least the one she was registered here under was Margaret Hornsby, not Stein."

H is about to interrupt and Oliver holds up his hand to stop him. He continues before H can say anything.

"You then land an identical plane and load three crates of, probably, ill gotten gains, and take off again. You then fly exactly seventy five miles and land in a field owned by a farmer, Mister (notebook again) John Morrissey. He doesn't grow anything in that field, it's just left to grass and occasionally some sheep are let in there to keep the grass at a decent length."

Oliver reaches into his pocket and removes a photo and places it in front of H.

H looks down at it. It is the barn where the plane is hidden. Or not so hidden now.

"Nice shed."

"It's a barn, and it's not empty is it."

"No idea, never seen it before."

"Well, I have been right up to it and there is a very nice airplane that is, amazingly, exactly the same plane as the one that was **supposed** to take my client's goods to Switzerland. I bet it once had the same registration as the plane that was forced to land by Trisha Kinchin's heart attack. Now what are the chances of that do you think?"

"Long I would think."

"Bloody impossible according to the aviation authorities. So, question one, who did it? Question two, where are the contents of those crates? And question three, when do you need to return the plane?"

Oliver leans back and takes a gulp of his tea. It is cold.

"Jesus, this is awful. How can you stand to drink this?"

"That's only one of the small things being in a home makes you accept."

"I can imagine."

"No you can't, you have no bloody idea. You come from a generation that think about themselves only. We, the old people who shaped your world and gave you a start in life, are now an incontrovertible pain in your collective arses. You will step on anyone to get what you want. Hence you being a parasite working for a snobby bastard who has lost a few quid and is whining about it."

"Harsh but fair, probably."

Oliver leans forward.

"I'm not here to shop you; I just need one piece of documentation back, that's all."

"Why?"

"Because that's what my client has asked for and will pay for. It's contained in crate number (again with the notebook) 946848. It is a box about yea big (he holds his hands out to show the size) wrapped in purple velvet. Seen it?"

Without reacting at all H replies.

"No."

"Well I'll just have to go on digging. You see, the reason I was hired is that I am like a dog with a bone, I don't let go. I never, and I really need to stress this, **never**, lose. I always get my man."

"Blimey, from Columbo to Wyatt Earp in three easy moves. Very impressive."

"No I'm not impressive. Dogged, unrelenting, annoying, and thorough, like a wasp, always in the wrong place at the right time, eventually. I don't give up."

"More like a tick I would say. Well good luck then."

H is about to stand and leave. Oliver decides one last shot.

"Look Mr Hitchcock, as impressed as one might be by your successful robbery and subsequent escape you have been rumbled. I, however, want to ask one question."

"And that is?"

"Why?"

H looks long and hard at Oliver Watts, Insurance Investigator, nice guy, nemesis. He decides the game is up but he's not about to go without a fight.

"Ok, I'll tell you. I'll tell you bloody why. Because every now and again I wake with a hard-on that would break bricks. Because I have a brain in my head that functions twice as fast as the Oxbridge educated, flash-suited, semi-literate morons who are overrated, overpaid and overdue to try and do a job that I spent thirty years honing to a skill level they could only dream of achieving and never achieve as long as they live. Ringo Starr and the other three Liverpool moptop squealers once asked 'will you still need me, will you still feed me, when I'm sixty four'."

H takes a deep breath.

"Well the answer is invariably no and fucking no. Now I don't believe in the afterlife, reincarnation and the power of Shirley MacLaine. I believe that this life is a one-off deal, no dress rehearsal, when you snuff it you're worm food or dust, so I decided that I could either curl up and die, turn into a lemonade guzzling, slipper wearing doom brain or I could shake myself up and do something to prove to myself and the rest of the world that I am still a functioning, living, breathing, active part of the human race. I do not want to be thought of as a dead head OAP, so this opportunity came along and I took it! Now I know what we did was against the rules but guess what, we all felt alive for the first time in years and not like some semi-castrated half-man that the world had put in a cupboard and forgotten."

Another breath.

"Ask me if it we would do it all again, even if we end up in the pokey and everyone will say a resounding, life-affirming, smile-driven................YES."

A smile from Watts.

H continues.

"But guess what Mister Watts, you have still got to prove it first and then find the evidence to prove that we actually did this thing and prove we had a plane and that all the other evidence is just circumstantial. The la-di-dah, hoi polloi rich gits can't tell anyone as they have been at it themselves. We aren't exactly buying rollers and furs now are we? Besides which, the police don't care and who is going to believe a group of old wrinklies like us could pull off a perfectly timed, well rehearsed, daring robbery? No-one that's who. The reason? Because everyone sees us as almost invisible, worthless, pointless old farts. But we *are* alive and we can still surprise the world every now and again."

Oliver Watts raises his hands and claps very slowly. He is starting to really like this crazy old guy.

"Bravo Mr Hitchcock, bra – bloody – vo. I don't give a monkeys about the other crates, I don't care about what's in crate 946 whatever, I just want the velvet wrapped box. Do you understand?"

H realises he's being offered a deal without it being said.

"Let me ask the others. Can we meet later?"

"Yes, I'm going to go and have a shower, I think I need one."

"You do."

"Thanks. I'll be back at three?"

"Ok."

Oliver Watts stands and turns to leave then turns back and puts out his hand to H. He looks up and extends his hand and they shake a firm, friendly, respectful handshake that speaks volumes.

He turns and heads for the main door. H sits and stares out of the window. He is still there forty minutes later when Trisha sits in the seat where Oliver Watts had been.

"What did Kojak want?"

"Columbo."

"What?"

"Kojak was bald and said 'who loves ya baby', Columbo was the one in the tatty coat who looked like a tramp but always worked out who did it."

"Whatever, what did the little shit want?"

"Amazingly, to do a deal. He wants one small box from one of the crates so he can get his reward money. I think he'll let us keep the rest."

"That's great, give it to him."

"Then that means admitting we did it and he could turn us in to the authorities."

"Oh I see, I hadn't thought of that."

"We need to have a meeting with everyone present. Can you get Gil, I think Gus is in his room, I'll get him and George, Olivia is in her room, we'll pick her up en route."

"Ok. Let's round them up."

Trisha stands and heads for Olivia's room. H heads off to the stairs.

Ten minutes later they are all crammed into number 68 faced by H and all waiting to see what's going to happen.

H is about to start outlining the situation when there is a knock on the door.

"We are all here, who the hell can that be?"

CHAPTER TWENTY NINE - COMPROMISE

H steps forward and puts his hand on the handle. He blows hard and turns the handle. Standing in the doorway is Oliver Watts. Clean shaven, nice white shirt and a decent suit a quick change and a shave in the back of his old beetle has brought about a massive transformation. No sign of the beige mac. Without asking he steps into the room. He sees everyone standing together Trisha, Gus, George, Gilbert, Olivia all side by side, H now behind him closing the door.

"Well, well, the Mild Bunch……or is it The Magnificent Six."

No-one says anything.

"Look, can we sit and talk about this situation?"

Still nothing.

"Ok, I'll talk, you listen."

Oliver takes a further step into the room. He feels six pairs of eyes all on him. He takes his notebook from his pocket and a small pen.

"Right. I have been hired by a certain Lord of the Realm to recover a small box that was supposed to be housed safely in Switzerland right now. He is a very determined Lord and as such has offered a very handsome reward. It is my job to recover it."

All six stand looking at him with their arms crossed, chins down, teeth clenched.

He continues.

"I have spent the last two weeks tracing back the actions that led to the audacious robbery of the crates that were to be sent to Switzerland. I must say that in the fifteen years I have been investigating robberies, scams, heists, blags whatever they be termed I have **never** come across such a well planned, well executed operation."

H bites his lip to stop himself smiling.

"This is what I know."

He points at Trisha.

"You and Margaret."

Trisha interrupts him.

"Mags."

He acknowledges the point.

"Mags and you went to Switzerland under pseudonyms Miss Sappho and Miss Stein, you went to Lugano and boarded a small Pilatus to Shoreham, two tickets at a cost of £5000 each."

He whistles.

"Now that's some price for a couple who spend their days in an old people's home."

Trisha clenches her fists to stop herself saying anything incriminating.

"While on the plane, Mags is taken ill but unfortunately dies. You then have a problem as the Captain decides to carry on to Shoreham. **You** then have a heart attack and the plane is forced to land in France. Great recovery by the way."

"It just requires a bit of a backbone and a stiff upper lip. Things you clearly know nothing about."

"Touché"

Oliver turns his attention to Gus.

"You rent a plane from a very greasy little man at Shoreham's main Rental agency." (he looks at his notebook) "Jupiter Aeronautics, who was expecting his plane back four days ago and is frantically trying to track down a very nice fifty five year old black gentleman, a Mr. Everton Weekes. Oh how much fun you must have had picking these names? Anyway, he was accompanied by a very attractive younger lady my little slimy salesman tells me."

He looks at Olivia.

"Well that just has to be you."

He smiles at Olivia and gets a cold stare in return.

"Slimy boy says he was impressed at the 'old fellas' pulling power. Nice touch that he thinks you were in your fifties."

Gus says nothing, just stares at him.

"This plane miraculously acquires the same registration numbers as the plane Misses Sappho and Stein are on and lands on time. It loads the crates on-board and takes off. Oh, an American couple, Marge and Arthur Kowalski complained that they were expected to share a plane with dangerous chemicals and had to take a plane almost six hours later to Switzerland. They are on a whirlwind European tour and are now on a coach tour of the Alpine villages between Lugano and Berne it took me four hours driving to catch up with them."

He looks at Olivia, admiration in his eyes?

"Your idea?"

Olivia gives him another very cold stare.

"So how am I doing so far?"

Silence.

"Then comes the clever part, the plane takes off, doesn't get into the airspace it needs to go International and then drops off the radar. It's not reported missing and no-one really seems to care."

H speaks for the first time.

"Except you."

"Well, not even me really. Just my Lord Moneybags, and ***he*** has put up a substantial reward to get his goods back."

He lets that statement hang in the air.

"Now it took me a while to figure out what happened to the plane and obviously the contents of the crate, or crates contained therein. It is amazing what you can find on the internet. So I spent many sad hours in my sad little office tap tap tapping away until I discovered a cracking site called Google Earth. Did you know that you can type in a post-code and the satellite will zoom in on your address. Amazing."

Once again he let's that sink in.

"But if you don't have the post-code you're reduced to searching, searching for a needle in a haystack. Or a barn in a big field."

Everyone stays silent and tries to look impassive as their world unravels.

Oliver continues, he has their attention.

"I decided that the plane had been hidden away somewhere but there must be enough space to land as well. In a one hundred mile radius there are seventeen fields on level ground with enough space to land a plane of that size and then only five that have a decent sized barn close by. It took four days driving around before I found Morrissey's farm. I found the plane."

H decides enough is enough.

"So what. There has been no report of a crime, no-one has called the police so, in the words of Mark Twain – 'If it's a miracle, any sort of evidence will answer, but if it is a fact, proof is necessary' – putting a plane in a barn is not illegal. Landing it in a field might be, so what. You have nothing. "

"That's not the point. I ***know*** what happened, I know you have the box Lord KnobHead wants back."

They all exchange glances.

"I want to put a deal to you."

Silence once again.

"Give me the box he wants and I will give you the reward money."

Stunned silence.

Olivia breaks it.

"Why?"

"Because my employer is a very annoying, very rich, upper class twit. He has offered me a large reward to offer to get his box back. You can keep everything else and split the reward. This will give you a real result and you still haven't had to give anything of value up."

Stunned silence.

George asks the question they all really want answered.

"How much?"

"Sorry?"

"How much is the reward?"

"Well, it's **One Hundred Thousand Pounds**."

Absolute silence.

Gilbert almost explodes.

"Fuck a duck."

Gilbert's exclamation somehow releases a valve in the room and they all start talking at once. H steps back and rests against the wall. His brain is racing. He is still thinking when he realises that they have all stopped talking and are looking at him.

H pushes himself off the wall. He looks at Oliver.

"So, what do you get out of this? How do we know we can trust you? What assurances do we get?"

Oliver looks at H.

"Good point. Right. We split the reward equally. We split the money from the crates equally. I will be an equal accomplice and therefore as at risk as you."

H weighs all this up.

"Seems fair."

Oliver smiles.

"And there is one more condition."

H looks at him with trepidation.

217

"What's that?"

Oliver turns away from H and looks at Olivia.

"I want a dinner date with Olivia."

They all turn and stare at Olivia as if she's done something wrong.

"What? I've got sod all to do with this."

She looks at Oliver.

"Why?"

"Because you are the most interesting, challenging, smart, funny and attractive woman I've met in many years."

Olivia blushes to her roots. A bright glow above the white of her uniform.

Gilbert takes the opportunity to get a dig in and makes out he's warming his hands on her red face.

Smiles all round.

"Well? Is it a deal?"

Olivia has one last glance round.

"Okay, but only for the good of the deal."

They all nod sagely and mutter their own thoughts about this turn of events.

As they are talking Oliver walks over to Olivia and stands right in front of her.

"Well?"

"I've said yes haven't I?"

"Good. I will hold you to this deal."

Olivia smiles beside her reservations. She is very attracted to this unusual man.

Oliver turns round and the others are all looking at him.

H speaks for all of them.

"Right, what happens next? We all seem to be in agreement. This deal is ok. What do we need to do?"

"I'll contact Lord Numb Nuts and tell him I have the box. I *do* have the box don't I?"

"We will get it. You get the money. In cash."

"Ok. Let's meet here again tomorrow morning and we'll set out a plan. I will draw up a document detailing my involvement so you have leverage when you hand over the box. I have one chance with this slippery git so we must get it right."

"Ok then, see you at ten tomorrow."

They all say their goodbyes and finally Oliver is leaving and turns to smile at Olivia.

"See you."

She smiles goodbye.

Oliver leaves and the team all slump down on the bed or against the walls.

Gilbert starts to laugh.

"Well bugger me, I never expected that."

"Well, now we are heading into unknown territory."

"Can we trust him?"

They all turn to Olivia.

"Don't ask me. I don't know."

H rubs his hand over his head again and again.

"Gus, you go check the crates, see if you can find this box but make sure Romeo has gone. We don't want him getting his mitts on the stuff before we get any money. The crate number is 946848. Gil, you go with Gus. George, me and you need to get back to the plane and have a double check that everything is ok."

Olivia raises her hands, palms up, level with her shoulders.

"What do I do?"

H smiles at her.

"Go get ready for you date!"

"Very bloody funny."

"All meet here at four this afternoon. Gus, Gil, after you check for the box, bring any cash from the crates carefully back to Gus' room. Use a small bag that can be zipped or locked in case anyone is watching. Do it bit by bit. We'll meet at Gus' at four and count what we've got from the crates."

They all know their jobs, so they leave and head off down the corridor. H checks out of his window. Oliver's beaten up old Beetle is no-where to be seen. He feels confident that Oliver is being straight with them but human nature is a funny thing where money is concerned.

H and George leave number 68 and head once more for Morrissey's farm.

CHAPTER THIRTY - REWARD

Gus and Gilbert check outside the windows from the lounge. No sign of Oliver Watts. They exit SummerVale and head down the lawn, past the pond and their workout area. The small path leads past the neat allotment with peas, beans, potatoes all sprouting and parked under the shade of a willow tree sits their white van. Gilbert takes out his keys as they walk towards it. Gus is carrying a small holdall with a check pattern. Gilbert opens the rear door and the two of them climb inside and pull the door shut behind them. Once inside Gilbert picks up the crowbar they left on the floor of the van and sets to work levering the lid up, it is much easier this time as the nails had been removed once before. Having taken the lid off they start opening the boxes and parcels. Bundles of money cascade out, twenties and fifties, tens and fivers. Some neatly bound in bank wrappers, some with elastic bands around them.

Gilbert can't contain himself.

"Bugger my boots there's tons here."

Gus begins to sing.

"We're in the money, we're in the money."

They stuff these bundles into the holdall until it is full. Silverware and   family heirlooms are all placed on the floor. Gilbert looks at the second crate; the number inked on the side is the one they're looking for. 946848.

He crowbars the lid off. More cash in packages, a beautiful silver flask with a crown on the front. Then a glint of purple. Gilbert removes the A4 sized box. The purple velvet giving the air of expensive treasure.

"Shall we open it?"

"No, let's wait. It's H's call. He put all this together."

"Ok, let's get back."

They climb out of the van, lock it up and Gus carries the holdall as Gilbert tucks the velvet box under his arm. They almost skip back to Gus' room. Gus empties his sock drawer and they stack the money in the drawer then lay some socks over the top.

"I hope your socks are clean."

Gus looks at Gilbert's sandal clad, sock free feet.

"At least I've got some socks."

Gilbert shrugs and they set off on the second trip.

H and George pull up behind the barn having driven around every angle four times to check for other cars and in particular a VW Beetle. Nothing in sight, really nothing, no cars, vans, tractors or people.

H walks up the doors and grabs the padlock. Undoes the lock with an audible click then pulls the chain through the handles. He pulls one side and George the other and they walk backwards opening the doors and reveal the small plane.

"Come on George, check everything outside, I'll do inside. Rub everything down. No fingerprints anywhere."

George sets off and immediately starts to rub the outside; H climbs into the plane and does the same.

An hour later and the completely dusted plane looks no different but is now absolutely fingerprint free.

H re-locks the barn and pockets the key.

"Let's get back. Lots to do still."

Oliver sits outside Lord Hunter-Brown's Mayfair residence. A four storey townhouse he uses as his pied- a- terre. He picks up the mobile phone and dials. The phone is answered almost immediately.

"You better have some good news for me."

"Good morning to you too."

"Fuck that gumshoe tell me what you know."

"Well, I have good news and bad news."

"What's the good news?"

"I have your box."

Lord Twitty squeals with delight.

"Yes. ….and what's the bad news?"

"The return of it will cost you one million pounds and it has to be done quickly."

"Fuck, shit, bastards. Are you trying to play me?"

"No, and to prove it I will waive half my fee. You agreed to pay up to one hundred thousand for the safe return of the documents, You agreed a fee for me plus expenses, that stays in place. The gang want to try and exploit every item they stole I can get you your documents but they want a million."

"So how do I do this? I can't get a million pounds out today. Will they take a cheque?"

"Hardly. I have a bank account number and sort-code. You transfer the funds and the box will get handed to me and I'll bring it to you. Ok?"

"I suppose so. What happens if I transfer the funds and then don't get the box?"

"Then my reputation is shot and you can tell everyone I'm crap."

"Oh big deal. I will be out a million pounds. Who did this? Who has my box?"

"A gang of villains with absolutely nothing to lose. They are fully prepared, fully resolute and think they are prepared to exploit these opportunities to the max."

"Oh shit. What am I going to do?"

"Ok, here's how I will play this with them. I will get the box delivered to the bank in a safety deposit box. You set the transfer up. We instruct the bank to swap the two items. Will they do that for you?"

"Yes. But I still don't like it. What if we get the box back and don't send the money?"

"You really don't want to be doing that. Remember, they know who you are and where you live!"

"Yes, yes, I see."

"Can we get this done tomorrow?"

"I'll call you back."

He hangs up and re-dials.

He gets straight through to the bank manager. He rattles off instructions to the minion on the other end of the phone following Oliver's instructions to the letter.

He calls Oliver back.

"Right, that's done. We can meet at my bank in Mayfair at noon. Ok?"

"Ok."

"And you just better have my box in the bank by then sonny."

Oliver doesn't bite at the continued putdowns.

"I will, don't worry."

"Good. Now please go and get my property."

The talking is over.

Oliver puts his phone on the passenger seat and bangs the wheel of his tatty old beetle then he calmly drives away and heads for SummerVale.

H and Gilbert drive back to SummerVale having double checked the plane. No sign of the barn being broken into, the plane still intact. They knock on Gus' door and Olivia opens it. As they walk in they stop stone dead. Gus' bed is smothered in bundles of notes, piles and piles of cash. Sitting atop the huge pile is a box wrapped in purple velvet.

H can't contain himself.

"My God. There's a ton of cash here. How much?"

Gus smiles back.

"Plenty."

"But how much?"

"No idea until we've counted it."

"Well what are you waiting for? Count"

As they move toward the bed H realises that Trisha isn't there.

"Where's Trish?"

Olivia replies.

"She doesn't feel so well. I think the strain of the trip and only a few hours sleep plus Mags has wiped her out."

They all dive in and start piling money up in little stacks. Olivia, having locked the door, joins in.

Almost forty minutes later and the money is tidily laid out on the bed.

H takes charge.

"Gus how much?"

"One hundred and sixty thousand."

"Olivia?"

"One hundred and forty thousand."

"Gil?"

Adopting a 'darts' voice.

"One hundred and eighteeeeeeey."

H smiles.

"And I have counted one hundred and thirty five thousand. Bloody hell..."

Olivia has been doing the maths in her head.

"Six hundred and fifteen thousand pounds. Bugger me."

"That's Romeo's job."

"Don't be filthy. But that's amazing."

"That's over a hundred thousand pounds each."

Whoops and cheers all round.

Gilbert bends down and kisses the top of one pile.

"And that's before we sell all the other stuff in the van."

H stands up straight.

"No, that all goes back in the crates and back in the plane. We take their money, no problem. We take heirlooms and possessions they care about then we have a big problem."

Gilbert looks a bit sheepish.

"Sorry H, you're right."

"Now, let's see what is worth a hundred thousand pounds."

H picks up the velvet covered box and removes the cover. The oak box gleams up at H. It is locked and H turns it over.

"Not very heavy. Must be papers."

"Smash it? "George offers.

"No, let's leave it intact. I don't care what's in here if it's worth a lot of squidlies."

Olivia runs her hand over the oak box lid as H holds it.

"Maybe Oliver should decide what to do?"

The four men pull faces at her.

"Sod off you lot. I'll go and see if Trisha is ok."

H picks up a large bundle of cash.

"No, I'll go."

He walks to the door putting the cash under his t-shirt. He turns at the door.

"Make a note that this is coming out of my share."

H taps on Trisha's door. A few moments pass then the door opens. Trisha sees it's H and stands aside to let him in. He looks at her. Red eyes, no make up, dishevelled hair. She looks terrible.

"You ok?"

Trisha tries to smile.

"Not really, no. Can't help thinking about Mags."

H walks forward and puts his arms around her.

"I know. But she helped us change all our lives. She died in a better place than rotting away here."

"I know but I just feel bad."

H reaches under his t-shirt and removes the wad of cash. He hands it to her.

"Well, this is what we did it for."

Her eyes light up.

"We made over six hundred thousand pounds Trish."

"But what about Mags' share?"

"We'll all live our lives for her from now on. That's a legacy no-one could ever better."

Trisha smiles. H smiles back.

"That's a nice thought."

"Come on, we need to celebrate. Big day tomorrow. Maybe."

Trisha puts the wad in her drawer and they leave her room.

In the lounge they all sit round a table. The team are all smiling, they are all thinking about the future. Oliver walks into the room and they all turn to watch him approach.

Oliver pulls up a chair and wedges himself in between Gilbert and Olivia.

"So, here's the news. Tomorrow at noon we will swap the velvet box for not one hundred thousand pounds but......da.da. da......one million pounds."

Sharp intake of breath from all around the table.

Oliver continues.

"I am to take the box to M'Lud's bank in Mayfair, his Bank Manager has arranged for a transfer to be made. His account with a million pounds for our account and safety deposit box and that's the deal done."

"Can we trust him?"

"Absolutely not. We must be very careful."

Silence.

"And you all must have somewhere else to go after this is all over in case he wants to try and get his money back."

H stands.

"Come with me" He nods at Gus.

"Come on."

The three leave and head for Gus' room, the others just sit around with their mouths open.

Inside Gus' room H hands Oliver the box. He holds onto one side as Oliver takes the other.

"Don't worry, I'm not going anywhere."

H lets go and Oliver removes the velvet wrap.

"It's locked."

"We know."

"Have you tried to open it?"

"No."

"Let me try."

Oliver takes out a small pouch and opens it. He takes out a small metal object and inserts it into the lock. A wiggle and a click and the lid pops open.

Oliver opens it and lifts the documents out. He unfolds them and glances at them one at a time. He whistles.

"No wonder he wants these hidden, His family were a bunch of thieves. I bet this would make interesting reading for a certain journalist."

"We don't care, just get them to the bank and let's get it over with."

"Okay, but I have an idea. Is there a photo copier in the building? "

"Yes, in Hailsham's office. Why?"

"Insurance."

"Come with me."

Oliver follows H out of the door.

Next morning Oliver delivers the box to the bank at nine thirty. He walks out of the bank and sits in his small car tapping the steering wheel. At five to twelve he feeds the meter and walks back into the bank. He waits for a few minutes and the manager approaches him.

"Mister Watts, the transfer is done. You, and you alone have control of this account. The other account now belongs to my client Lord Hunter-Brown. I believe that concludes our business. You are a very wealthy man how can the bank help you with your finances?"

"It's not mine, trust me, where it's going will not be of any interest to the bank. Can you make out six cheques to cash for £150,000 and one for £100,000. I'll take them with me."

"Of course sir."

Oliver sings all the way back to SummerVale, every now and again he pats his pocket and his smile grows.

Having arranged to meet in H's room he is not surprised when he taps on the door and it is almost flung open by H. Oliver steps in and has a very solemn face on.

"Sorry guys, we got turned over."

An outburst of 'I knew it, what happened, bastard, damn' from the team. Except Olivia who walks right up to Oliver and stands inches from his face.

"I don't believe you."

The team all stare at the spectacle in front of them.

Oliver stares back but can't keep it up. He grins from ear to ear.

He reaches into his pocket and removes a white envelope, he hands a cheque from inside to each of the team and finally gives one to Olivia who hasn't moved. As he holds up her cheque she raises her hands to take it and he kisses her gently on the lips. She closes her eyes and doesn't pull away.

The team all applaud and everyone looks at their cheque in amazement.

With the shared cash, each member has just over a quarter of a million pounds.

H opens his wardrobe, takes out a bottle of champagne. Pops the cork and pours a measure into plastic cups.

He raises his and everyone does the same.

"Here's to the future."

H looks at Trisha, Olivia looks at Oliver. Gilbert raises his eyebrows and looks at George lovingly.

Gus laughs out loud.

"Arhh you make a lovely couple."

They all start laughing, a very happy group of thieves.

CHAPTER THIRTY ONE – AFTERMATH

The Virgin airline 747 banks and turns to descend to the runway at V. C. Bird International Airport on Antigua. Olivia, happy in the window seat, turns to Oliver and smiles. The idyllic golden fringed island almost smiles back up at them as the plane swoops down in the sunshine.

A short time later they are waiting to pick up a hire car from ***Dion's Car Hire Emporium***, an exercise that takes an hour longer than the same job in the UK as the sales executive Clive (as his badge proclaims) insists on offering his advice on at least twenty places to visit, the best beaches to go to and how to get there. In short, they receive a guided tour at no extra cost but so far they haven't even left the airport.

Once in their small rental car they drive along Sugar Factory Road and head for Curtain Bluff. As they approach their destination each turn of the road reveals an even more beautiful view.

Olivia is awestruck.

"My God, it's like paradise."

"Let's hope he's here."

They drive to a small sandy parking spot and stop the little car. They get out into the furnace that is Antiguan sunshine. Olivia stretches like a cat relishing the warm sun.

Oliver points at a white house a hundred yards to their left. They walk up to the picket fence and a sign outside states that they are at a house called **SUMMERVALE** . Olivia shakes her head in laughter. They walk to the porch and ring the bell. No reply. They ring again. No reply. Olivia walks round the side of the house and follows a little winding path past a garden full of exotic plants. Oliver follows just behind her.

They walk to the beach that is at the bottom of the garden and spot two striped deck chairs right by the sea. A 35 foot motor boat is anchored by a small jetty nearby; the nameplate reads "*Crime Pays*". They walk across a patch of sand and obviously make a noise as Gus' face appears round the side of the deckchair. A huge grin appears on his face; he is wearing a baseball cap and looks no older than fifty. He stands and a young man stands behind him.

He hugs both Olivia and Oliver in turn then turns to the young man.

"Olivia, Oliver, I'd like you to meet my son, Derek, he's here for a holiday."

"Pleased to meet you."

Handshakes all round.

Derek, a very polite young man looks at the two white tourists.

"So how do you know my Dad?"

Oliver replies.

"Oh, we did a job together a while ago and became friends."

Gus likes the explanation.

"Yes, a lifetime ago."

Sitting at her cramped desk in The Independent office, Charlotte Green is handed an A4 jiffy bag by the post boy. She leans back and rips open the top strip. She peers inside and removes a sheaf of documents. The Coat of Arms on the top of a clearly photo – copied sheet catches her eye, she flicks through the rest of the papers getting more and more excited. She looks inside and on the back of the jiffy bag, no note, no return address, nothing. Just a wealth of information. She starts to read more closely. She begins to bounce up and down on her seat. Her rotund sub editor watches intently and slowly walks to her desk.

"Anything interesting?"

She spins on her seat.

"Graham, you won't believe this lot. We have all the evidence we need to run the Lord Hunter – Brown expose. He's buggered, it's all here, original land registry, pay-off receipts, everything. He's buggered."

She clenches her fists.

Graham senses her excitement and gets caught up in it.

"Write it up, call the lawyers and we'll run it in Sunday's magazine, if it is all you crack it up to be you'll get front page as well."

She jumps up and kisses him on the cheek.

"You lovely fat man. We are going to destroy that pompous, snotty, smug, self-centred dirt bag."

"Watch it you, I'm a finely tuned athlete."

She sits back down and starts to read again.

Suntanned and relaxed Olivia and Oliver alight from the train at Exeter Station in Devon. Their hire car is waiting and they set off toward Chulmleigh. They drive for two hours, pottering around the beautiful Devon countryside until they arrive at

Chulmleigh. A few enquiries and they head out of the small town and arrive at a stone arch with a handsome wooden sign that reads **EASELEIGH.** They head up the driveway and in the fields to the left and right, fields full of poppies and daisies they spot people with easels, paint brushes, palettes all painting different aspects of a beautiful house in the distance.

They pull up outside a rambling cottage, a big country cottage and the door opens and George comes out. He is wearing a white smock top and a beret and both have paint splashes all over them.

He throws his arms out wide.

"Welcome to Easeleigh, artist colony and refuge."

They all hug and head indoors.

The Ryan Air flight lands at Cork Airport and once again Olivia and Oliver climb into their rental car and head out of the airport. The rain has finally stopped and the light is amazing. Heading up country toward Tipperary they follow instructions and turn off onto a small single track road in the direction of a large hill, not quite a mountain but high nonetheless. The winding track leads them to a collection of caravans, huts, tents, a community outside the real world. They park the car and walk through a grassy area, children playing, a man strumming a guitar smoking a very large spliff. They hear a shout and turn to see Gilbert dressed in a purple kaftan, wearing sandals and a headband walking towards them.

He hugs them both.

"Welcome to freedom. This is Magic Mountain. Me casa su casa."

He takes their arms, one either side and leads them towards a group of people sitting under a large tree.

The drive to Gloucestershire takes a little over five hours, then a further hour to find the cottage they are searching for. They park up outside just as the light begins to fade putting the picture postcard cottage into shadow. They walk to the door and it is opened before they can knock by Trisha. She looks twenty years younger. Smartly dressed, casual but classy. Hugs all round and they go inside.

Trisha leads them into a comfortable lounge.

"I'll go get H; he's in the study working."

Olivia and Oliver watch her go and take a seat. They hear a noise, footsteps on floorboards and H appears, he hurries round the sofa and hugs them both.

———————————

The table is full of empty dishes and three empty wine bottles. The four friends very relaxed in each others company. Olivia sips her wine.

"That was lovely Trish, thanks. This is such a lovely house."

"Yes, we love it. Nice and quiet. Lots of lovely walks. Peaceful."

H nods in agreement.

Oliver joins in.

"Don't you get bored?"

H replies.

"No, we have plenty to keep us going. Lots to do in the garden. Besides, we have had enough excitement for one lifetime thanks."

They all chuckle at the recollections.

Oliver stands.

"Little boy's room?"

H points down the corridor.

"Last door on the right."

Oliver sets off. As he walks down the corridor he looks at the paintings on the wall.

"Lovely artwork you've got."

H shouts back.

"All from George, he has found some great painters down in Devon."

Olivia cocks her head to one side.

"He's been here?"

Trisha answers.

"Yes, a couple of times. Lovely to see him so happy. Like a regular Vincent Van Gogh…"

"With both ears."

Oliver walks on and is about to open the door to the toilet when he glances to his left. The door has swung open and he sees inside. A table lamp illuminating two large pin boards mounted on stands. A collection of photographs of a beautiful hotel. A4 sheets with scribbled notes. Timetables. Cuttings from newspapers. Pictures of paintings. Valuations. Oliver realizes that H and Trisha are preparing another job.

"You crafty old sods."

He steps back out of the room and heads for the toilet shaking his head and smiling.

The End

Printed in the United Kingdom by
Lightning Source UK Ltd., Milton Keynes
137657UK00001B/118-135/P